THE ORGANDY CUPCAKES

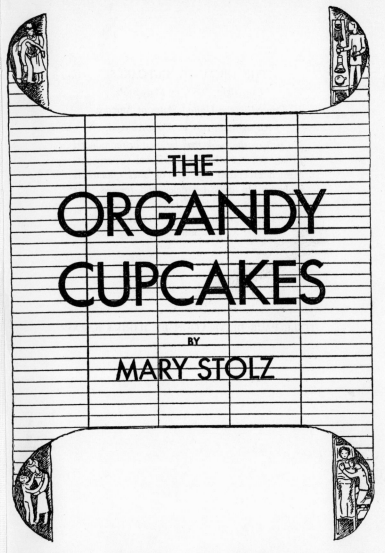

THE
ORGANDY
CUPCAKES

BY

MARY STOLZ

HARPER & BROTHERS PUBLISHERS NEW YORK

THE ORGANDY CUPCAKES

Copyright, 1951, by Mary Stolz

Printed in the United States of America

TITLE PAGE DECORATION BY ILONKA KARASZ

To My Husband

THE ORGANDY CUPCAKES

Chapter 1.

"If there were dreams to sell,
Merry and sad to tell,
And the crier rung the bell,
What would you buy?"
BEDDOES

ALL afternoon the May sunshine had darkened till the tree-tops moved in a yellow aquarium light. Presently it would rain—on the old Sibert Memorial Hospital, its new east wing, on the Nurses' Residence, the surrounding acres of trees and meadow, on the broad river that flowed on the west.

Two student nurses were talking idly, one on the path that led to the Residence, one at the window of the second-floor Utility Room, their subject a fat gold spaniel who lay upon the grass in lolling sadness, tethered to a low iron fence. Property of Miss Merkle, Director of Nurses, Dollar spent much of his time so chained on a three-foot leash that offered no scope at all for dog pursuits. Rebellious at first, he had at last settled into dumb resignation that scarcely appeared to recall tail-wagging as a function of enticement, or satisfaction.

Nevertheless, Rosemary Joplin leaned her forehead against the screen, the better to see him, and thought she detected wistfulness in his limp pose.

1

"Oh, go ahead and pet the dog, will you?" she asked Gretchen Bemis, who shrugged and shook her head.

"I'm not talking to that dog's people," Gretchen explained.

"You don't have to take it out on him, do you?" Rosemary felt that if Gretchen wouldn't scratch those disconsolate ears, she'd have to run down and do it herself.

Gretchen wouldn't. She leaned against the iron fence and smiled, saying nothing. A beautiful girl with immaculate shining brown hair, Wally called Gretchen a "Dresden girl with a red-plush heart." And Wally, one of Gretchen's innumerable men, was more or less the designer of this scene. He'd gotten Gretchen back late from a date, and Miss Merkle had removed two of her late-night privileges. So now Gretchen wouldn't pet Miss Merkle's dog.

Rosemary, committed to seeing that Dollar got petted, frowned. Why it should matter now, when for weeks at a time she barely saw him, was immaterial. At twenty, she was still prey to the young practice of making herself mental promises and then having to carry them out. It was, she thought, just another version of avoiding the cracks on the sidewalk or having to count fifty people from the train window before being able to read. She sighed with relief as Gretchen moved out a white-shod toe and gently massaged Dollar's disorderly ears.

"Feel better?" Gretchen asked, whether of Dollar or herself, Rosemary wasn't sure. Moving away from the iron fence, Gretchen slanted a smile up at Rosemary, who was inside and on duty while Gretchen was outside and off.

The low cry of the ambulance preceded it along the circular uphill drive that led to Emergency.

Gretchen, with a flick of the hand, turned away. She was heading for the Residence but took a circuitous path through the garden. In the pond goldfish swam toward the surface of the water, restless mouths agape, then turned with an almost hinged motion toward the pebbly bottom. There were broad lily pads in the pool, pinks and periwinkles around the border. Gretchen sat on a stone bench, watching the fish, thinking that she liked this time . . . the coppery stillness before rain. She wished there were time for a swim at the Y before Dr. Bradley's class. It had been a very tiring day.

She'd assisted in the morning at one of Dr. Alvord's operations. A thyroidectomy, a patient of Dr. Whitney's, and she'd heard one of the observing students whisper to another that the patient had a cardiac involvement and what if his heart couldn't take it? Dr. Alvord had snapped out, "Whitney says it's safe." And that had completely been that. Then, less than halfway through the intricate, delicately precise operation, a large figure, masked and gowned, had entered the operating room silently and stood by, a motionless intent observer. Dr. Whitney, staying with his patient even when, strictly speaking, there was no need to.

There was a time when Gretchen had considered doctors the most godlike of creatures. She'd been sixteen when her father went to the hospital to have his appendix removed, and Gretchen, in constant attendance, had discovered interns. She made up her mind then that she wanted a doctor for her very own, but discarded as impossible the idea of finding him in an office. For one thing, she was too healthy. For another, even granted some reasonable complaint, you could hardly shop from office to office without arousing suspicion. Finally, from all she could gather, doctors simply treated and released you. She'd never heard of one, except in the movies, falling in love with a patient. Barely possible, but largely improbable. So, short of hurling herself under a bus, she could think of no other way to guarantee a good long hospital stay except to become a nurse. She went to college for two years in her Ohio home town, then entered Sibert Memorial on a sort of medicine-man hunt.

That had been a long time ago, and her conception of doctors had undergone changes. But whatever their faults as a group, individually they had, almost without exception, a quality Gretchen cherished. They had purpose.

Now Wally, she thought, does not. Unless you wanted to call his aberrant fancy for studying dead cultures a purpose. He's like, she decided, the young gentlemen in turn-of-the-century novels—insulated. The other night when his car broke down, he'd been simply delighted at the idea of a subway ride to the end of the line. Imagine! Of course, he'd then called a taxi instead of taking the trolley as most people would have to do. Enough, said Wally, is enough. And he was not in the least concerned that he was making her late. She'd been so annoyed that she made a racket sneaking in the recreation-room window, and old Mew had swooped out of the dark like a horned owl on a chipmunk, and there she was, caught.

Well, room in the world for men like Wally was rapidly disappearing, and the best that could be said for him was that when the time came that there was no room at all, he would leave with grace. Only you need more than elegance and good sportsmanship in a man. You need . . . purpose.

A large drop splashed beside her on the stone bench in a crablike pattern. Another fell on her starched apron. The pool began to dimple. Gretchen jumped up, started for the Residence, then went back again to see if Dollar had been taken in.

As Gretchen left, Rosemary turned to the sterilizer, toed a pedal to lift the great lid. Removing basins through a cloud of steam, she shuddered, with the clammy heat, at recollection of duty in the Emergency Room. Well, that was over, for her.

4

She'd gotten through it. Though close to fainting more than once, she hadn't. But never, never would she work in an Emergency Room again. She was used now to the dying and the dead. Death could be cruel or compassionate, reasonable or insanely premature, but it should in some way give notice. Rosemary hated the Accident Room more for its suddeness than its violence. Death that leaped. Because you decided to cross the street to look in a florist's, walk downstairs rather than use the elevator, reach for the switch to get a bit more light in the bathroom. . . . For such casual, alterable decisions to mean that now you live, now you die. . . .

She stacked basins noisily as the ambulance slid, siren slowing away to silence, into the porte-cochere beneath her. Without thinking, she covered her ears so as not to hear the short pound of running feet, rubbery glide of the stretcher, low, decisive voices.

Miss Merkle looked in the Utility Room. "Miss Joplin, if you've finished the sterilizing, I believe your hands could be more usefully occupied in the wards than over your ears."

Rosemary gave a quick startled glance over her shoulder. "Oh. Yes, Miss Merkle, I'm coming."

"Is there something wrong? Your head ache?"

"No. No, there's nothing wrong, Miss Merkle. It's a little warm in here."

In silence, Miss Merkle managed to say that it was warm everywhere and covering the ears was a poor method of cooling off. Her own spare figure, immobile face, wings of grizzled hair, offered no quarter to heat or nervous students. She glanced around the room, found it orderly, moved out in the hall, followed by Rosemary. "If you'd help with P.M. care in the ward. . . ." she said, leaving. Rosemary, thinking of Dollar leashed to the fence, almost called after her that it was going to rain and the dog would get wet, but it might sound more like currying than concern. She said nothing.

5

Obstetrics was nearly always a good place to work. Patients who were young, pain behind them and nearly forgotten. For the most part it was a room of radiant women who didn't mind being awakened in the middle of the night, who thought the students in their striped blue with white bibs were nice, not, as many in other divisions regarded them, bungling inferiors with uniforms to distinguish them from real nurses. They were women who conversed happily with each other of loving, rearing, living.

There was sometimes, of course, Mrs. Parker, or someone like Mrs. Parker, who lay in a corner bed, silent, running a thin hand now and then over her flat stomach as though hoping to encounter once again the bulk that had been her baby to come. Mrs. Parker's baby had been stillborn three days before. She'd lain since in a shocked and cheerless silence, unreached by the nurses, her doctor, her perplexed and constant husband. Well, there was, now and then, a Mrs. Parker. Sometimes she'd lost a baby, sometimes added one to an already overfull family, sometimes, worst of all, she'd had a baby who wasn't . . . right. But the O.B. Ward was a nice place to work in spite of her. And that, thought Rosemary, entering it, is probably what they mean by becoming "casehardened." I'm casehardened when I can pity that thin still woman when I'm with her and forget the moment I leave. In time, she decided, she might even grow used . . . might possibly. . . .She pushed away the thought of the ambulance whining up to Emergency. It was no concern of hers, not now.

"Oh Miss Joplin, there you are how nice to see you," said Bed 1, Mrs. Tarrant, who always ran her words together, presumably in order to get more said, though she already talked more than anyone else Rosemary had ever known. A verbal cataract. "You're on this afternoon now isn't that nice," Mrs. Tarrant flowed on. "Because I've been telling my husband

6

about you how pretty you are and since I'm leaving soon I hope you'll get in to meet him. The very prettiest I told him, except Miss Gibson, of course," she added, naming the only other nurse in the room, Nelle Gibson, a squarish dun-haired student whose room was next to Rosemary's in the Residence. Nelle was not nearly so pretty as Rosemary, a sylph with yellow short swirled hair, and neither of them was the very prettiest, this distinction going quite obviously to Gretchen Bemis. By some standards, Gretchen might be considered too plump. But then, Gretchen set her own standards and might very well, Rosemary thought, revive the grand manner with her magnificent full figure, her long hair that went up in thick braids the color of mahogany. One of the interns, it was said, had called her "Bemis de Milo." The girls were skeptical. "Those interns never see a student nurse," they said, "so how would they know what one of us looked like? You put Elizabeth Taylor in one of these uniforms, and the boys wouldn't notice if she turned up under a microscope." Rosemary said nothing but was inclined to believe the story, because uniform or no, if Gretchen wanted to be noticed by a man, and she generally did, why that was all there was to it. She got noticed. No hiding her light under a butcher apron.

Mrs. Tarrant had moved on to the subject of her other children. ". . . absolutely not I told her, if my son says he didn't nobody's going to tell me he did and would you believe it Miss Joplin she actually went ahead and said yes he did, so I said I'm not taking your word for it and if Petey says he didn't what you say doesn't matter and my husband says so too, but of course really Mr. Tarrant didn't know a thing about it because manlike he always says maybe Petey's wrong which shows how much he knows about it, I wonder how they're getting along without me Mr. Tarrant says the house seems like a tomb. . . ."

It probably does at that, Rosemary thought, setting a basin

7

of water, towel, soap, and washrag on the bed table. If you've lived with a riveting machine most of your life, you'd be bound to notice its loss, which doesn't mean you'd miss it. She smiled, nodded, said, "Mmm," as she brought basin and so forth for the next bed, because Mrs. Tarrant had suspended action, indicating that now it was someone else's turn to speak.

"*Just* what I thought," Mrs. Tarrant resumed quickly. "And what in the world poor Maureeny is doing without her mother I just hate to think why that child. . . ."

She puts a "y" at the end of everyone's name, Rosemary thought. The children were Petey, Jacky, and Maureeny. The husband's name, she knew from the records, was Albert. She wondered whether Mrs. Tarrant called him Alley.

"Do you suppose she calls Mr. Tarrant, Alley?" she whispered to Nelle in passing.

"Dearie," Nelle said.

Mrs. Parker never appeared to hear anyone's conversation. She kept her pale eyes fixed on the window—on the glass, not the trees outside. Docilely she accepted a basin of water, washed her face and hands with slow strokes.

"Do you think we'll have a storm?" Rosemary asked, looking out attentively at the yellowing light and languid branches.

Mrs. Parker turned her head, fixed lusterless eyes on Rosemary's mouth. "I don't know." She wiped her hands, lay back against the pillows.

Rosemary tried again. "Perhaps you'd like your bed a little higher? I always think it's fun to watch a storm come. Or perhaps you'd like a nap? I could lower it, if you like." Her voice sounded chattery in her own ears, but she couldn't simply remove the basin and go on, with no attempt at all to draw this woman back, for a moment, from the stone-still world into which she'd withdrawn.

"All right," Mrs. Parker said.

8

All right, what? Higher to see the storm? Or lower to nap? Mrs. Parker wouldn't care. She would look out the window or go to sleep, whatever the position of her bed indicated. Well, higher then. Cranking the bed up a few notches, Rosemary straightened an unruffled spread, admitted defeat, went on to the next patient who, after a quick glance at Mrs. Parker to be sure she wouldn't notice, smiled gaily.

The patients were washed. In the large bathroom, Nelle and Rosemary filed away cups and basins in labeled cubbyholes. Eight cubbyholes for eight patients, their names written on adhesive tape to signify brief ownership. The strips of adhesive had been changed so often that all the paint was flecked off.

"You get any reaction from Mrs. Parker?" Nelle asked.

Rosemary shook her head.

"Her poor husband. He's just about wild." Nelle sounded impatient. "All very well for her to brood about the baby, but what about him?"

At the sound of a man's voice in the ward, the two students hurried out in order to be attentively, silently, present as the first of the doctors began evening rounds.

It was young Dr. Grafton, the newest medical intern, on his first round in O.B. He was accompanied by Mrs. Mew, head nurse, who frowned at the two girls, suspecting they'd been wasting time gossiping in the bathroom, then turned her attention to Dr. Grafton. Mrs. Mew's attention was on a sliding scale. A great deal for the big men, the surgeons, the solidly established obstetricians. A bit less for younger or more obscure private practitioners. Still less for residents. Almost none for interns. Since Dr. Grafton was new to Sibert and fresh from training, he rated the absolute minimum. Mrs. Mew's air of unspoken superiority had been known to drive interns to stumbling speechlessness, to red-faced anger, to apathy. Few of them were indifferent. Rosemary bit her lower lip and felt a reluctant admiration for Miss Merkle, who might be stern but could never be called petty, who extended the same precise courtesy and respect to every doctor in the hospital.

It would have surprised the patients to know that the hospital pivoted not round them, but the doctors. Patients came, stayed, died, or walked out. But the doctors were always there. Sibert had four residents, eight interns, an occasional influx of student doctors to whom everyone paid as little attention as possible. Between Mrs. Mew's and Miss Merkle's attitudes fell the average manner of the nurses toward the medical men, most of them prepared to give respect where it was due, with an extra fillip of zeal for the really big wheels.

Rosemary watched nervously as Dr. Grafton approached Mrs. Tarrant. She hated to see anyone humiliated, and Dr. Grafton didn't look very stalwart. He was tall and slight and blond. When he smiled, as he was smiling now at Mrs. Tarrant, his eyes almost closed. A very nice smile.

Nelle nudged her. "He's wearing a clamp," she whispered.

Rosemary, with regret, had already noticed. It was an affectation limited almost entirely to interns, the wearing of a Kelly clamp dangling from the breast pocket of the white uniforms With the necessary stethescope sticking out of his hip pocket, Dr. Grafton looked almost too well equipped to serve. Mrs. Mew had a malevolent way of fixing her eyes on the clamp rather than on the doctor's face. Her manner indicated that, without the clamp, she'd certainly have taken him for an orderly.

Nelle and Rosemary watched, wishing him well, as Dr. Grafton addressed Mrs. Tarrant.

Scarcely waiting to hear his greeting, the patient in Bed 1 shot off on a torrent of words, the main current of which concerned a headache and Petey who had not done whatever anyone said he had. Mrs. Mew waited confidently for Dr. Grafton to sink beneath the flood. He listened for a few minutes with every appearance of interest, finally lifted his hand in a slight gesture of abeyance. And it was a slight gesture, barely a turn of the wrist. Mrs. Tarrant closed her mouth, and silence fell.

"Now, I don't quite understand, Mrs. Tarrant, what it is that Petey is supposed to have done that you say he didn't."

Mrs. Mew was openly astounded. Rosemary and Nelle, standing with hands folded behind their backs, exchanged glances. To their knowledge, it was the first time anyone had ever inquired exactly what it was that Mrs. Tarrant was talking about. The idea had been to endure her volubility as long as necessary, and then duck. Now even Mrs. Tarrant seemed surprised at the turn things had taken. She hesitated.

"Well, doctor," she explained slowly. "You see this neighbor she says Petey's a bully and chases her kid around like not letting him come on our block and stuff like that. . . ." She stopped. Apparently with her audience assured, her words were less so.

"Surely that isn't all?" the doctor encouraged.

"All? Well, Petey says he didn't chase the kid and this neighbor says Petey's lying, we had an awful brawl her and me right out on the street and I hate that sort of going on. . . ."

"It's been worrying you since you've been here?"

"Something awful doctor, because to tell the truth," she lowered her voice, "I ain't sure if Petey's lying or not and then there's Maureeny all alone at least not with me. . . ."

"Look, Mrs. Tarrant," the doctor interrupted (no slight feat), "you are going to have to stop fretting about things this way, or you won't be in any condition to take the new baby home and attend to him properly. Then you'll have to start worrying all over again," he smiled. Rosemary noticed that he even knew the sex of the baby. She looked at Mrs. Mew to

11

see if that complacent being were at all impressed. Mrs. Mew, however, was wearing her "new-broom-wait-till-he's-been-here-a-while" expression, her superiority unrelaxed. If anything, she was a little haughtier, implying that a good doctor would have better things to do than idle with a talk-heavy ward case.

Dr. Grafton seemed unaware of Mrs. Mew's disdain or the students' approval. "You're supposed to be getting a rest here, you know," he went on to the patient. "Isn't there someone home taking care of the children?" Mrs. Tarrant admitted that her sister was on deck. "Well, as long as you know they're in good hands, you just forget everything but getting yourself rested up. You'll have enough to do when your little vacation is over. And as for Petey . . . well, Mrs. Tarrant, all children lie at times. It's a strong defense weapon for the young. They learn the value of taking their medicine and standing up to things later on. The thing for parents to do . . . is just try to understand. Set a good example, of course," he smiled, half turning away. He looked back to add, "I've never in my life heard of a boy who didn't chase smaller boys at some point in his career. You forget about the children, Mrs. Tarrant. Just take it easy for the rest of the time you're here. And we'll give you something for the headache."

He went on to the next bed, leaving Mrs. Tarrant silent, bemused, and somehow contented. Rosemary hadn't realized before that Mrs. Tarrant had always been frowning as she talked. The Tarrant forehead was quite smooth now.

Mrs. Mew turned suddenly on the two students. "Aren't you girls due at a lecture?" A complete dismissal. Reluctantly they deferred, departed.

"Well," said Nelle as they went through the great glass doors that walled Maternity from contact with the corridor, "Kelly clamp or no, that is some doctor."

An operative case was wheeled around the corner on a

stretcher. The patient was talking earnestly to an attendant and white-capped surgical nurse who accompanied him. His eyes were brilliant, from excitement, or drugs, or perhaps both. Rosemary turned her head a little, a gesture of compassion. She wondered if the man was frightened. Men often were, more than women, who seemed, actually, to take some pleasure in the trip to the O.R. (Gretchen had once said that it was because men just naturally got attention all the time, whereas most women couldn't get it without going to extremes.) As they approached the elevator where the stretcher waited, the man's voice, high and rapid, reached them. Rosemary tried to give him a glance of sustaining comfort, but he was too busy talking to notice.

"And they say Snead can't putt!" he complained. "Why, man, I've seen him sink an eighteen-foot putt like it was eight inches. . . ." The elevator arrived, doors opened, stretcher slid aboard. The patient's turbaned, sheeted figure disappeared, protesting the skill of Snead as the elevator rose.

Nelle glanced sideways at Rosemary who smiled hesitantly. She knew Nelle and Gretchen thought she dramatized too much, but there was no way to explain the rush of compassion she felt for the patients, whether or not it was welcomed.

"Wait a minute," she asked now, realizing that it was raining. She rushed into the Utility Room, looked out the window. Dollar was no longer there. Apparently Miss Merkle hadn't forgotten him after all. She went back to Nelle.

Chapter 2.

DR. BRADLEY was speaking to the seniors in the little lecture room, the one facing the garden. The room was nearly full, the lecture nearly finished. Dr. Bradley was unique because she induced no sleepiness in a group of students beginning to feel hungry. They listened with almost the attentiveness they'd give a morning lecture.

". . . So, you'll see that, as a premature infant needs every gram of energy he has, merely to remain alive, the amount of handling he can endure is not to be compared with that given a full-term infant. Naturally, following a feeding, it will be. . . ."

Dr. Bradley wore a grey flannel suit, a scarf of red and black clasped by a large filigree gold pin, soft black-leather pumps. The red of her lipstick matched the scarf. She was vastly admired by the students for her ability, for being one of the most successful pediatricians in town, for her beautiful clothes.

"Though why," Nelle complained, "They always specialize in pediatrics. . . .We need trail blazers, women surgeons, women neurologists, women. . . ."

But, "Give them a chance, will you?" Gretchen interrupted. "They have to eat, don't they? They've only started in the medical field, and you can bet your last artery Dr. Alvord isn't moving over to make room for a hen. Or at least not on his operating table," she added reflectively.

They liked Dr. Bradley because she was a good teacher who seemed to care whether or not her students learned something. Many of the doctors simply stood at the front of the lecture room, opened their mouths, talked upon their subjects for forty minutes, closed their books, and left.

"That," said the ever-militant Nelle, "is because they're afraid the nurses will be too well trained. The average doctor thinks a nurse should stand beside a bed with a thermometer in one hand, an emesis basin in the other, and nothing at all in her head. What a doctor thinks a nurse should be and what nurses are trained to be have absolutely no relation to each other."

Gretchen sort of agreed with that.

Now, listening to Bradley, Gretchen thought she looked entirely too young and handsome for a woman doctor. Idly, she speculated what Dr. Bradley, had she not chosen to be Dr. Bradley, would be doing instead. Seeing a properly elegant husband off on a late commuter's train, dropping a couple of sturdy children at a private school, whisking off to the club for nine holes before luncheon. The picture presented itself so easily that for a moment, only a moment, Gretchen pitied the doctor for the woman she might have been.

Nelle listened with passionate concentration. It took her about double the listening and studying that Gretchen required to get precisely the same information. Briefly she flashed a glance at Gretchen, abstractly studying the cut of the doctor's suit. It really didn't matter what Gretchen fixed her mind on. When it came to exams or, for that matter, to handling a premature baby, she'd know just what to do. The distribution of grey matter, Nelle decided, was wretchedly unscientific. Here you had a girl who wouldn't use a tenth of her brains probably, yet that tenth would serve her as well as another's furious application of every cell. Hastily, she swung back to Bradley.

Rosemary listened but looked out the window. The rain wasn't so heavy now, but the tulips and pansies were drenched and weak. Tree trunks glistened darkly, and from all the young leaves pear-shaped drops quivered and fell through lavender air. Beside the window a few branches of lilac hung heavy blossoms and wet polished leaves. She couldn't smell them, for the window was closed. Yet, looking at them, she almost knew the sweet wild tang of the purple clusters against her face. Fragrance does have a memory, she thought.

It was odd that Dr. Bradley still spoke of methods—procedures of feeding, handling, nursing. This was, after all, the last lecture of her course. Rosemary would have thought the subject would be . . . well, broader, more philosophic. She turned from the window toward the speaker who now leaned against the desk, closed a book with lingering deliberation.

"And now," Dr. Bradley resumed, "a few additional words concerning not only infants but children . . . and you. I think there is little I can say concerning the profession you've chosen that others won't say, and better. It's a good profession, but you all know that or you wouldn't be here. What I would like to mention is a phase of it, the field in which I work. Some of you, and I know because I've heard the discussion not only among women doctors but among nurses, feel that women who become doctors elect Pediatrics because it's the field most open to them. And at present that is quite true, though the picture changes daily. For my part, however, I'm in Pediatrics because it's where I want to be, because I believe that children are the most important people in the world, and the pleasure, the privilege, of knowing and helping them is not replaceable. It's quite possible that some of you will be pediatric nurses. Heaven knows, it's a sphere that has room as well as challenge and opportunity. It is a matter of general opinion now that any patient must be considered in the light of more than his pathology. His home, his background, his aspirations, all these bear on his treatment. Not so long ago the only reason a patient opened his mouth was for the insertion of a thermometer. Today we ask him to talk first and strip later. To tell not only his mother's maiden name, but as much as he can of his relationship with her. Not only his business address, but what that business is and whether he is happily adjusted to it. The importance of such material in a case history is generally recognized.

"But consider how much more delicately we must move with a child, who is usually resentful of his illness, bored, annoyed, or frightened by direct questions about it, and more inclined to talk generally than specifically. As nurses, whether in private homes, institutions, or Public Health, you would have invaluable opportunities to glean specifics from generalities. Some of your findings *could* make the difference between a truly healed child and a merely discharged one.

"In conclusion, I suggest that there is more to a patient than can be read on a thermometer and more to life than can be seen with the eyes. That applies not only to the nurse or the doctor, but to all of us, people together, keeping our eyes open, but what is more important, our hearts."

After dinner, as Rosemary opened the door of her Residence room on the fourth floor, white eyelet curtains lifted inward. In the gentle half-dark, the room had a waiting quality, pale-blue bedspread and rug smooth and clean, glass-topped bureau neatly arranged with a few bottles, a picture of her mother who each year looked more and more a girl.

Not turning on the lights, she sat on the window seat, looking toward the back of the hospital, the treetops floating in the gauzy rain. The air had deepened almost to purple, air with a sweet warm freshness that moved against her face. Across the garden, lights in the hospital windows glowed with smudgy outlines. She could see figures moving. White one in an upper room—nurse adjusting screen. Portly grey-clad gentleman pacing back and forth—patient registering boredom. Near the ambulance entrance, two orderlies leaned on the rail where Gretchen had stood in the afternoon. The glowing paths of their two cigarettes sprang and dived as they smoked. It was very peaceful. That could almost be an apartment building over there, not a hive for ailing bodies. But the lights were on behind the great top-floor windows of Surgery. She could see by the gaping doors that the ambulance was out again, could hear in her mind the monotonous voice of the loudspeaker summoning this doctor, that doctor, to Surgery, to O.B., to the telephone.

No, the illusion of peace didn't stand up well.

Dr. Orin Whitney stepped through the doorway of Emergency, stood talking to the orderlies. Even in the dark, Rosemary knew it could be only Dr. Whitney. No one else carried such height so casually. Watching him, she thought of the time she'd first seen his now so familiar figure.

It had been during her first year. He'd come out of a patient's room, looking not at all like a doctor. More, Rosemary decided, like a prize fighter. Six feet three, with a sort of pushed face, he came in shades of tan and brown. Brown hair, eyes the color of coffee, brown suit and tie, tanned skin. There was an air of great, but somehow unaccented, physical power in his walk.

"Who's that?" she asked the nurse at the desk.

"Why, that's Dr. Whitney," she said in the tone one might use for, "Why, that's St. Peter" or, perhaps, "Laurence Olivier."

"He doesn't look much like a doctor."

The nurse gazed upon the broad retreating back, smiling

dreamily. "You know," she said, "he was an intern here when I was a student. During the war, that was." She seemed lost in thought. Rosemary tried to look encouragingly interested, succeeded, because the nurse continued. "The first time I saw him was in the elevator. Mrs. Smalling was in it too," she said, naming the long-incumbent chairman of the hospital board of directors. "And you have no idea how Mrs. Smalling can behave, or have you? Anyway, she was even worse in those days, when the turnover of doctors in residence was terrific, and most of them were refugees from abroad. She sort of constituted herself Hostess America, welcoming them with the air of 'aren't you fortunate, you poor specimen, that I, Mrs. A. Dexter Smalling, am pleased to be gracious to you in the name of this generous country.' Really, I sometimes wondered why one of them didn't push her downstairs. Anyway, Dr. Whitney got in the elevator, and I guess she'd never seen him before either, because she took one look and went into her act. 'Well, doctor,' she says, 'and how do you like America?' Dr. Whitney stared at her and then smiled and said, 'Very much indeed.' She accepts that, nods, and says, 'And this hospital? I hope you realize the many opportunities you will have here and are taking advantage of them?' 'All I can,' says the doctor. That sort of stopped her for a minute because she didn't know how to take it, but I guess the urge to patronize is pretty strong, because she went on and said, 'And are you from Vienna, doctor?' 'Philadelphia,' he says. I tell you, I thought she'd shoot through the top of the elevator. I don't think she's ever liked him since. But if she doesn't," the nurse added, suddenly brisk, "then she's the only one. Well, come along. Miss Merkle says I'm to supervise while you do a colostomy dressing."

Dr. Whitney was in general practice now. Still young enough to answer night calls, popular enough to keep the large practice he'd inherited from Dr. Gardner Wylie, good enough to have to devote most of his free time to clinics. About his only relaxation was to play tennis three or four times a week with Preston, the gardener. Or push the roller, which seemed to be a form of relaxation.

Rosemary glanced over at the tennis courts. No one had thought to take in the nets. They sagged like great pale webs in the darkly advancing twilight. Where the lights of the Residence touched it, the iron fence gleamed wetly, the rest of it melting out of sight. Preston was supposed to keep the courts rolled and marked, but sometimes Dr. Whitney helped him, the two of them laughing as Dr. Whitney pushed the heavy roller back and forth like a toy. Preston was a good match for Dr. Whitney's game. More afternoons than they rolled or marked, Preston and the doctor would slam through two or three hard sets. Dr. Whitney had a light supple bounce that took him all over the court, but Preston's serve was a splendid thing, the second as accurately powerful as the first. After their game, Doctor Whitney would pull on his sweater, mumbling that men their age should begin to think about golf. Preston just laughed.

Preston was nice.

"Miss Joplin," he would say, looking up from a border of portulaca and pansies idling beneath budding gladioluses and spiked foxglove, "did you know that foxglove is blooming digitalis?"

And Rosemary, feeling the glow of unaccountable pride that Preston's attention always produced, would shake her head, though as a matter of fact she did know it.

"Yup," Preston would nod. "You couldn't ask more of anything. Beautiful and useful. But you'll notice. . . ." He'd be getting up from his knees now, "You'll notice that it isn't quite as handsome as the ones that exist just for being beautiful. Flowers have got these things pretty well arranged."

Mrs. Mew found Preston deficient in respectfulness, which surprised no one. Deficiencies had a way of running up to Mrs. Mew, demanding notice and publicity, which she duly gave them.

Thinking of Mrs. Mew reminded Rosemary that the room was very dark now. She switched on the light, started to remove her uniform. She'd take a shower and then drop in to see Gretchen, who wasn't, she'd bet, reading a Materia Medica.

Gretchen wasn't. She was propped on her bed in a plaid housecoat, her thick shiny hair disheveled, eating peanut brittle and reading Edith Wharton.

Her room was not like Rosemary's. It was a good deal like Gretchen—dashing. The bedspread grass green, the rug red as a fire engine. On the wall hung a pastel by Loren MacIver of Emmett Kelly, "The Hobo Clown." It was a dark picture, with a rosy flare on the bulb of nose, thick chalky lips around a red upside-down smile, and deep, drooping, almost indiscernible eyes.

When Rosemary knocked and entered, her glance flew, as it always did, to the bright green swag flaunted at the window top. It was a piece of material left over from the bedspread that Gretchen had looped between two brass rings. The curtains below it were marquisette dyed red.

Gretchen looked too, as though wondering if it were still there. "Gay, isn't it?"

"It's like living in a Christmas tree." Rosemary dropped to the yellow armchair. "Have you seen the new intern, Dr. Grafton?"

"No. What's he on?"

"Medical. That's right, you're still in the O.R."

"Tell me about Dr. Grafton."

21

"He's . . . nice. You remember Mrs. Tarrant, the one I told you about who talks all the time? Well, he asked her what she was talking about. I mean, asked as if he really wanted to know and then paid attention to the answer. It seems she's been worried to death about her family ever since she came, so he sort of talked her out of it. Talked her out of talking too, apparently. When I left there, she was just sitting with a slap-happy smile on her face."

"Enterprising man. What's he look like?"

"Tall, but awfully thin. A blond. And you know," she said with sudden recollection, "when he smiles, his eyes practically close."

"That's always attractive. Maybe it's why he does it."

"No," Rosemary said slowly. "I don't think so. He doesn't seem. . . . I hope he's going to be on O.B. for a while, because he simply reduces Mew to shreds."

"How?"

"Well, he doesn't do anything actually. He doesn't seem to know she's there. Not rude, just too busy for her." Rosemary fell silent. She had been going to mention the Kelly clamp so they could be amused together, because she did like the feeling of shared laughter with Gretchen. Now, for no obvious reason, she was reluctant to discuss Dr. Grafton any more.

"I wonder if Nelle will go in the Indian Service, or down in Kentucky, now," Gretchen said.

"I wouldn't be surprised. She's in such a hurry to start."

"Start what?"

"Living?" Rosemary wasn't sure.

"Oh, for heaven's sake. I can't understand people like that. She'll never enjoy anything if she keeps wondering only about what's coming next."

"That's better than just not enjoying things at all."

"Who's that?"

"Me."

Gretchen took a bite of peanut brittle, tried unsuccessfully to wipe her fingers with a tissue. It shredded and stuck. Finally she popped the fingers in her mouth and licked them. Noticing Rosemary's eyes on her, she shrugged. "I ought to give up peanut brittle or have hot water piped in. It seems to me you enjoy things. I mean, perhaps not as much as some people, but then. . . ." She'd been going to say that there was no reason for Rosemary's not enjoying things, but after all, how did she know? "Why did you go into training?" she asked curiously. She had, actually, often wanted to ask that, because Rosemary didn't seem to fit here. She took everything too hard. Rosemary was odd in many ways. She was, for one thing, prettier than she looked. Her hair was very nearly yellow, her figure very nearly perfect. But she spoiled a nice face with that look of . . . brooding, was it? Apprehension? Perhaps the look of someone who'd simply wandered into the wrong orbit and would be perfectly all right somewhere else. "Why did you?" she repeated.

Rosemary shook her head from side to side. "Because a girl I knew was going to, I suppose." She sounded uncertain.

"What girl?"

Rosemary smiled a little. "Well, she's gone. Couldn't take it." She thought a moment, then added, "I'm going to take it, though."

"Is it really that hard?"

"It isn't easy. Do you think it's easy?"

"No. But I never thought of stopping. I like nursing. Parts of it, anyway." Rosemary didn't reply, so Gretchen went on, "Haven't you ever thought that perhaps you'd be better off doing something else? There are so many. . . ." She broke off at the pinched look on Rosemary's face.

"Gretchen, don't."

"I'm sorry."

Rosemary leaned back, scratching her fingernail along the

arm of the chair. "It's just . . . Miss Merkle asked me that too. I had such a horrible time convincing her that I should stay. Just hate to have it brought up again, that's all."

"But why convince her? If you. . . ."

"Because I've got to finish, that's all," Rosemary interrupted. "Anyway, I like parts of it, same as you do. Not the Accident Room. But I've gone too far. . . . Quitting's so bad, Gretchen. Worse than being afraid, I think."

"So long as you're sure . . . which one would be worse for you, I mean."

"I am."

"Then that's fine. I'd hate to see you leave. Nelle says she decided to be a nurse after she'd read that Ernest Poole book about the R.N. mounties. I suppose she saw herself mounted, struggling through an icy dawn over Satan's Gulch Lick . . . cold cliffs, desolation, perhaps a vulture now and then . . . the rude mountain cabin where she would deliver the baby, probe for feudin' bullets, bear the message of vaccine. . . ." Gretchen was laughing a little, carried away by her own words. "Oh, hi, Nelle," she said. "Come on in."

Rosemary turned. Nelle was poking her head in the door. "Are you talking about me, Gretchen Bemis?" She came in, serene and dowdy in an old wrapper.

Gretchen nodded. "I'm telling Rosemary why you went into training."

"Because I wanted to be an astronomer, only it was too hard," Nelle said. "Can I have some peanut brittle? Did I tell you what mother said about trichinosis?" she asked Gretchen.

"What?" said Gretchen warily.

"She said, 'Trichinosis? A *terrible* disease. And do you know how you get it? From those little sausages they give you at cocktail parties.' "

The three of them burst into laughter. "Mother majored in

24

art and eurythmics," Nelle explained. "She's really not at all sure what we're studying. Certainly not why."

"Who is?" Rosemary asked.

The other two waited.

"At that, I suppose you two are," Rosemary admitted with a shrug.

"I just want to be a nurse," Nelle said simply.

"I'm not sure what I want to do after we graduate," Gretchen reflected, "but I know why I'm here."

"Well fine. You're both very lucky. I don't know why I'm here or what I want to do. The only thing I'm sure of is I'm going to finish."

Gretchen thought it wasn't the best attitude. But one way or the other, Rosemary had managed to make herself a good nurse. So probably it didn't matter too much what her reasons, or lack of them, were. She reached for another piece of candy.

"You're going to get fat, if you eat all that," Rosemary said.

"I'm trying to forget tonight's so-called dessert. You could knock a house down with that sponge cake." Rosemary got up. "Are you leaving?" Gretchen said, getting off the bed.

Rosemary nodded. "I'm sleepy. You don't have to see me to the door," she smiled. "Night, everybody." She went out, closing the door behind her. Gretchen sat in the yellow chair. She lit a cigarette after offering one to Nelle unsuccessfully.

"What's the matter with her?" Nelle asked suddenly.

"With Rosemary? I don't know, Nelle. I'm no psychologist." She stared at the wreathing smoke. "Sometimes I think perhaps losing her mother so suddenly was bad for her."

"Bad for her? Well, I should think so. But . . . it's awful, of course . . . only it does happen. That was six years ago, wasn't it? You'd think she'd be a little better by now."

Gretchen said she didn't know again. "It sends some people right into a tailspin, a thing like that. And then her father

25

marrying so soon again. Rosemary doesn't like her stepmother."

"It wasn't so soon. Two years. I think Rosemary's selfish. It isn't as if her stepmother was . . . oh, well, someone to be jealous of. After all, from what I hear, her mother was a ravishing beauty. The present Mrs. Joplin is hardly that."

"It's beyond me. I feel sorry for her sometimes." Gretchen stubbed out the cigarette, looking across the garden to the lights of the hospital.

"Sorry for whom?"

"Rosemary, of course." Gretchen thought a minute. "For Mrs. Joplin too, come to think of it." She moved her arms back in a lovely stretching gesture. "Nelle, if you could choose any time in history to live, when would you?"

"Now," said Nelle comfortably.

Gretchen laughed. "I'd take the Middle Ages . . . Harry, England, and St. George."

"Dr. Alvord said all the knights were dwarfs and the ladies-in-waiting had rickets."

"Why did he have to mention it at all?"

"It turned up in an anatomy lecture. You didn't hear him?"

"I must have been absent, thank heaven."

"I shouldn't have told you."

"That's all right. Nothing Alvord has to say could bother me. He'd find fault in heaven. But golly, what a surgeon."

"Yes. He's good. I suppose it's no wonder they act that way. I wonder what it's like. . . ."

Gretchen groped for her meaning, caught it. "Putting all the shreds and pieces together?" Nelle nodded. "They're not wiser or more skillful than the others . . . the internists, the pathologists."

"Surgery's showy, I guess that makes the difference," Nelle yawned. "Too bad about your late nights, Gretchen."

"Oh, well. I didn't have anything planned, really. But Mew is so annoying. I wish she didn't live in the Residence."

"If she hadn't caught you, someone else probably would have."

"I don't mean just the catching. She seems to get such pleasure out of it."

Nelle shrugged. She went out so rarely herself that Mrs. Mew constituted no threat to her leisure time, but there was no denying how she prowled and peered about for infractions of this or that. "You're lucky she reported you to Miss Merkle instead of the Board."

"The Board? For a half-hour's lateness?"

"It wouldn't have surprised me."

"It would have surprised the Board, I bet," Gretchen said.

After Nelle left, Gretchen lay a while in the darkness thinking about the hospital. Perhaps because she was to leave it so soon. If you don't work in one, she thought, you don't think of it till something is wrong, and that's the way it should be. But the hospital is a world. A watchful, wakeful world. It's basic. Where living begins and is prolonged and ends. Whatever its imperfections, and sleepily she admitted that there were many, the hospital means something. And that, she decided in a half dream, is more than can be said for some of the other worlds that make up the World.

Chapter 3.

THERE were fifty-nine girls in the nursing school at Sibert. They had wanted to be nurses, and their reasons were many. A few almost noble. The majority, just practical . . . a nurse could always get a job, couldn't she? Some, because there wasn't any reason not to. And some, more than would admit it, because they had thought it would be glamorous.

Well, they'd worked. Long hours, broken hours, dark hours. They'd seen a lot of people suffer and a good many die. With whining, courage, stoicism, or fright, the sick of the town had filled their days and nights.

They'd worked in the wards, where you could be ill for next to nothing; in private rooms, where you could spend a lot of money to have the same thing; in the out clinics, where the patient's time was squandered, the doctor's at a premium; in the grey-tiled, glass-roofed operating room, where miracles of grace and timing that rivaled any dance were endlessly performed. They'd spent hours with perplexed and tired children who didn't want to be ill, with nervous women who refused to get well. They'd gone into the tenement squalor where asepsis was a pan of boiling water and a fresh newspaper, where more often than not a new baby was just one more too many and had, almost from the beginning, to fight for his right to be. They'd wheeled convalescents to the sun roof, sheeted figures to the morgue.

They worked and worked and worked. And so discovered that there was room for nobility, for practicality, that there were reasons to be a nurse.

But glamour. . . .

Chapter 4.

GRETCHEN'S alarm rang at six in the morning from the other side of the room. This was a device. More often than not it worked, since, if the unremitting burr failed to rouse her, a neighbor's heel on the wall and bitter cry would manage to. Bitter words in the morning were as inevitable as day itself in the Residence, and as little noted. The most coldly regarded person was the occasional one who persisted in being hearty before breakfast. There had even, the year before, been a senior who, upon arising, skipped about trilling "Fresh as a Daisy," heedless of the poached eyes that followed her progress. Gone, thank heaven.

Gretchen, before breakfast, was a stately automaton. With unthinking precision she fitted herself into a uniform, brushed and braided pounds of hair at a slow unswerving pace. This morning, having made her bed, she stepped into the hall, closed the door with deep deliberation, somnambulated down the hall.

Across from the elevators, Nelle, in a bathrobe, was at the telephone, holding the receiver away as though she were examining the issuing words. What she saw seemed to perplex her. When the instrument grew silent at last, she lifted it cautiously back to her ear.

"Now look, mother," she said, "You'll have to give me some idea of what it's all about. I can't get time off to go haring across town if you really don't need me. . . .But I. . . .Yes, of course I would, only. . . .Oh, mother, all right, I'll ask Miss Merkle, only I don't see why you can't tell me. . . .If nothing's happened to you or Dad and the house hasn't burned down, it can't be so bad. Yes, I'll ask her. . . .Mmm. Bye." She hung up, yawned widely, started down the hall after a nod to Gretchen, who considered using her voice long enough to ask what the stir was, then decided she could always find out some other time.

As she stepped into the elevator, Nelle called suddenly. "Isn't this Wednesday?"

Gretchen didn't hear because the doors had slid together.

The Residence dining room, with sunshine ladling through mullioned windows, was a cheerful place. With its wainscoting of rosy tile, upper walls painted blue, its creamy drapes and blue-topped tables, the effect was one of pleasant brightness on even the sleepiest eye. Selecting tray and silver and proceeding along the counter to a table, Gretchen issued somewhat from lethargy. She sat near the window, conveyed a glistening prune to her mouth, then lowered the spoon cautiously as a thought, her first of the morning, emerged, full-blown and hideous. With a low cry, she half-started from her chair, sank again.

A student across the table studied her dismayed face a moment. "What's the matter?" she asked curiously.

Gretchen looked up, eyed the other a moment in silence. Then in a dazed tone answered. "It's my day off."

The girl looked puzzled. "But you're all. . . ." She checked herself as the situation became clear. "You mean you got ready for. . . .You mean you *forgot*?"

Gretchen could do nothing but nod. The enormity of the mistake seemed to take her breath.

"You better hurry right back to bed," the girl advised her earnestly.

But in a few minutes, Gretchen, who'd been drinking coffee to calm herself, began to find it rather funny. "No. I think I'll. . . .Well, what would you do, if you were awake at six-thirty with nothing to do?"

"Go to bed."

Gretchen smiled, returned to her breakfast. Really, it was quite silly. But she wouldn't go back to sleep. She had two cups of coffee, lounging in her chair with a sybaritic delight in the luxury of having nowhere to go and nothing to do. In the pleasure of the moment, she considered doing this now and then on purpose, quite aware that she'd do nothing of the kind.

Presently the night nurses began to straggle in, a sight so depressing that Gretchen hurried away, afraid to brush the bloom from this queer morning happiness.

Upstairs she encountered Nelle hurrying down the hall. "I tried to tell you it was Wednesday," Nelle said, pausing. "How in the world could you make such a mistake?" She sounded breathless. "Are you going back to bed?"

"No. I haven't decided. But not that."

"I don't suppose," Nelle said hesitantly, "I don't suppose you'd want to come home with me. We could give you a good lunch."

"I thought. . . .Didn't I hear you talking with your mother about some family crisis?"

"Yes. But you know mother has crises. Often, I mean. I think it's terrible of her to get me over there today. I sort of hoped Merkle would say no, but she said it would be all right if I work Friday. Please come along. We could settle the crisis and have lunch and then maybe go to a movie." Her voice brightened at that.

"All right," Gretchen said. "Only I hope your mother doesn't mind. Maybe we'd better call her first."

"Oh, no, it'll be fine." Nelle was now so buoyant at the thought of company for the catastrophe, which would probably turn out to be a broken dinner platter, that her round face glowed. "My mother," she said, accompanying Gretchen into her room, "has no idea of duty. How many times poor Dad has had to drop everything and come running because mother saw a prowler in broad daylight or some such thing. And then when the prowler turns out to be some poor man rushing for a bus, Mother can't understand why Dad *fusses* so. After all, it *might* have been a prowler, mightn't it?" Unconsciously her voice assumed Mrs. Gibson's inflections.

Gretchen, reaching for a beige gabardine suit and brown blouse, had a sudden impression that, behind Nelle's urge to toil heroically in the West or South, there could be a wish to fly to ills that she knew not of, rather than bear the ones she had.

"You look nice," Nelle said, honestly admiring, when Gretchen had pinned a brown felt flower to her lapel, slipped into alligator pumps and pulled on a pair of white-kid gloves. Nelle looked, as she did in everything but a uniform, like a pile of boxes dressed up. The stiff flare of uniforms tapered her squareness, but a silk print, such as she wore today, with a short red coat, emphasized every chunky line. Still, Gretchen reflected, as they rode downstairs, Nelle had a shiny eager look infinitely more attractive than some of the pretty-fluffy creatures you see.

They walked down the hill from the hospital with a delicious sense of flight. Nelle, because she shouldn't be off at all, Gretchen because in the ordinary course of things she'd be asleep for hours yet. They had checked out at the board, left Nelle's phone in case someone called, for Gretchen naturally, and were now, at seven-thirty, on their way.

In the trolley, Nelle began to wonder what it could be that would get her mother to a phone at slightly past six in the morning. Her voice had been chittery and high, but that was not unusual. She'd said something not very coherent concerning shame and living it down. But that made no sense, because her mother might be a bit lightheaded, but she was most decorously aware of what people say and would never, while conscious, give them a chance to say it. Well, they'd know soon enough. Meanwhile, it was fun to be out, nice that Gretchen had come along.

The steel wheels of the trolley made a most satisfyingly unhushed racket. In the hospital the idea of quiet prevailed—this despite an appalling amount of clatter from dropped basins, high voices pretending to be low, elevator doors that shrilled and jangled, bells summoning nurses, loud-speakers summoning doctors, ambulance snarling in and out. You could make and hear a lot of noise, but it was by common consent ignored and considered nonexistent.

But here! The motorman wrenched a cord that produced clamor every few minutes for no obvious reason, the coins shot with a merry ring into the coin box, the door slammed open, slammed closed, and everybody talked too loud. It was splendid.

Gretchen, next to the window, was pleased to see that just as she'd suspected a very brisk business of living went on at this hour outside the hospital. Lots of people scurrying about like . . .well, there was no avoiding it . . . like ants. She wondered why a thronging street invariably summoned up the image of ants. Never grasshoppers, or June bugs, or anything but ants. With a benign philosophy born of the amber early morning, she decided it must be because ants, supposedly, have a mission. And a mission, even if it consists entirely of carrying lumps of things larger than you are from one place to another, makes for bigness. People have a passion for bigness. Therefore, ants.

"Look at all the people," Nelle said.

"Lots of them, aren't there?" Gretchen prodded, hopefully. Nelle didn't disappoint her. "Like ants, aren't they?"

"Certainly are," Gretchen said cheerfully.

Most of the stores were still closed, but here a shopkeeper

swept his walk, there another unlocked a door. On the sunny side of the street, a cat on finical feet walked from an alleyway, bearing herself grandly, quite as though she were not a thin and wasted creature looking for a meal.

At one stop, a policeman swung aboard. He lounged near the motorman and read a paper. "Lookit," he said suddenly. "Here's a fellow won thirty thousand dollars on a two-horse parlay yesterday afternoon. Boy. . . ." He sighed. "Oh well, can't take it with you."

The motorman clicked his tongue. "If I can't take it with me, I'm not going."

That struck Gretchen as very funny. She laughed aloud, and the motorman, catching her eye in his overhead mirror, winked.

At the Gibson's very nice house, they had barely time to step on the porch before the door flew open, Mrs. Gibson flew out. "Nelle!" she cried. Then, seeing Gretchen, stepped back. "Oh. Oh dear, I didn't mean I'm not glad to see you, Gretchen dear. It's only. . . .Oh, how am I ever. . . .Well, we'd better go in. And you'll just both of you, being sort of professional and all that, you'll just have to look at this thing in a calm scientific light. The thing is not to lose our heads and go off half-crocked. . . ."

She bustled them into the hall, voice rising and falling like the song of a mosquito. It was a lovely center hall, rugged with springy grey broadloom. A blue bowl of yellow tulips stood on a console table beneath a mirror. At the far end, glass doors opened on the garden. Gretchen half-listened, half-leaned toward the house, which she loved. Raising her head to sniff the always-present fragrance of faint verbena, she flared her nostrils suddenly. There was a very strong odor, and it was not verbena. It was, she decided with astonishment, insecticide.

She realized that Mrs. Gibson had stopped talking, was simply staring at her, and that she must look like a spaniel about to flush a covey. "Excuse me, Mrs. Gibson," she said painfully, "I. . . ."

But Mrs. Gibson spread her hands, a gesture of despairing resignation. "Well, now you know." She ran into the living room.

Nelle and Gretchen followed in confusion, Nelle turning her head from side to side, snuffing noisily. "What in the world is it?" she asked her mother, who was on the couch, flapping a handkerchief at her bosom.

"I, oh, it's too awful. . . ." Mrs. Gibson's voice rose again. Suddenly she shot from the couch, whirled on it, pointing an accusing finger. "Perhaps even there!"

Nelle patted her mother's shoulder and stared at Gretchen, who could only stare back. Quite unexpectedly, Mrs. Gibson grew calm.

"Well," she said. "What am I going to do?"

"About what?" Nelle asked.

Mrs. Gibson drew a deep breath. "About the bedbug," she told them, lifting her head as though awaiting a volley of shots.

"Here?" said Gretchen.

"Here," said Mrs. Gibson.

Nelle sat down. "Is that why I asked Miss Merkle for the day off?"

"After all, dear," said her mother. "I do feel you're responsible."

"Me?"

"Well, who else? Heaven knows, I can't do anything about possible germs coming from that hospital. But when it's something as big as a bedbug, I feel you must assume your share of the burden. What am I going to do? I'll never understand why you couldn't have gone to Miss Worcester's." Her voice was mournful. Miss Worcester's, it implied, would harbor no transient bedbugs.

36

"Are there lots of them?" Nelle asked.

"Lots? You're mad. Do you think I'd still be here if there were lots? But I saw one." She turned to Gretchen. "I hardly like to say this, because I know of course that I can trust you, but this won't go any further than us three, will it, Gretchen dear?"

Gretchen shook her head. "Not a word," she said solemnly. "But one bug isn't very many. Maybe it accidently got in with the wash."

"No." Mrs. Gibson was decisive. "No, they're never alone," she explained, rather as though she'd made a study of the familial habits of bedbugs. "They go about in *tribes*. . . ."

"But the place smells like a Flit factory," Nelle protested. "What did you do, drown it?"

"What could I do? I found a can of insecticide, but no spray, so I put it in the syphon. . . ."

"Dad's soda syphon?"

"There wasn't anything else. Besides, it deserves him right for being away at such a time. It does seem to have a rather heavy spray," she admitted absently.

"I don't think Dad will approve. Where is he?"

"In Rochester." Mr. Gibson traveled in oilcloth and was away from home a good deal. "Do you think I should call?"

"Oh, mother, no. Look, if you're really worried, all you need to do is call the exterminator. Then you go over and spend the night at Aunt May's, and tomorrow it will all be forgotten."

Mrs. Gibson reflected. "Are you sure?"

"Of course I'm sure. I'll call for you."

"Well. . . .Well, all right. You call, and I'll make you girls some breakfast. Corinna's away, with her uncle the retired seaman, you know. I'll just whip up some batter, and we'll have waffles and bacon. Goodness," she called over her shoulder as she trotted kitchenward, "I've been too nervous to eat a bite. So nice to have you, Gretchen, darling. How are your dear par-

37

ents?" Mrs. Gibson had never met Gretchen's parents but knew they must be fine reliable people as they came from Ohio, such a sensible state.

Nelle called the exterminator, who agreed to show up that afternoon, and wasn't, as Mrs. Gibson had feared he would be, the least bit shocked.

Breakfast was on the flagstone terrace beside the garden, Gretchen eating as much as the others who hadn't already breakfasted. The sun seemed simply to recline on flowers, blossoming cherry trees, white linen, golden waffles. In its light, tiny drops of oil glinted on the surface of hot coffee, prism colors wavered in rounds beneath their glasses.

"There's a marvelous new intern on O.B.," Nelle said as she pushed her plate back a bit.

Gretchen looked up with interest. "I know. Rosemary told me about him."

"Oh? What did she say?"

"That he has a nice smile and a way with talkative women."

Nelle hadn't noticed the smile, a fact which made her mother sigh, but admitted that he definitely handled Mrs. Tarrant beautifully. "And, oh my, how he did rile Mew," she said blissfully. "She stared at that Kelly clamp till I thought it would bite her, but he never noticed at all. . . ."

"Rosemary didn't say anything about that. Does he really sport a clamp?"

"Well, after all, he's just come up from a Medical Center, and I suppose with all those people around you couldn't tell an intern from a Good Humor man," Nelle interpreted kindly.

Mrs. Gibson went to answer the phone, returned to say it was for Gretchen. "A man, dear. Lovely voice. Consider my home your own if you wish, only I don't know what you'll do about the smell." Mrs. Gibson had always been expansive with Gretchen and Rosemary. So far, Gretchen had been the only one to provide her with romantic interest. What in the world was wrong with Rosemary and Nelle, she couldn't understand, having been an indefatigable belle in her own youth and aware of no other reason for being young and female than to spend as much time as possible with those who were young and male.

It was Wally on the phone.

"Gretchen girl?" he questioned. "What are you doing abroad at this hour?" When Gretchen reminded him that it was almost ten, he said he'd hardly dared phone the Residence till now, thinking she'd be still asleep. "Thought for a moment the girl at the switchboard was having me on when she said you'd left by seven-thirty. What are you doing?"

"Having breakfast," Gretchen said, thinking Mrs. Gibson would not want her domestic problem mentioned.

"Don't they feed you at the hospital any more?"

"Not so well as they do here. Did you want something special?"

"Nothing except you. Now, now," he said as Gretchen drew a breath of protest, "You asked. What I had in mind was, the car's fixed, so I thought you might like me to take you away from all that. Didn't know you'd take yourself away. And at such an hour."

"Would you like to come over here? Mrs. Gibson says the house is mine."

"You mean spend the day?"

"Oh, no. Nelle and I were going to a movie after lunch. But if you'd take both of us, we'd go where you like."

"No day for a movie, certainly. All right, I'll be along in about an hour. Say hello to Nelle for me. That was her mother I was talking to, wasn't it? By the by, what's the address? Wait a sec. . . . 247 Camilla—Camilla Drive. Righto."

Gretchen warned him to come round the side to the garden rather than ring the bell, thinking it a way to keep the shame of the Gibsons *sub rosa*, and they hung up.

Nelle was delighted at the idea of an afternoon with Wally.

"But are you sure he wants me?" Feeling obliged to protest, though she'd have wept at any answer but Gretchen's, "Oh sure. He asked especially."

"What a nice young man," Mrs. Gibson decided aloud.

"Awfully nice," Gretchen agreed with a little too much emphasis, as though Wally were something she'd contracted to sell. "He's a dilettante, really. Travels about interminably getting passionately interested in all sorts of things, provided they aren't modern or alive. May I walk around the garden?"

Wally arrived in less than an hour. Beautifully barbered, round frame draped in grey flannel, he came round the corner, an anticipant smile hovering on his lips. He met Mrs. Gibson like a courtier, saluted the girls festively, set the air crackling with good temper and prospects. Mrs. Gibson, who, after all, wasn't going anywhere but to her sister's, and that in ignominious flight, brightened as though party-bound. Nelle was laughing as she poured coffee, a positively capricious laugh that widened Gretchen's eyes. Wally had that effect on people very often. He even had it on Gretchen, only not so dramatically.

"Tell me, Gretchen," he said, leaning forward to place his cup on the table. "Are you at all interested in Egyptology?" His voice wasn't hopeful.

"Hardly at all."

"Too bad." Wally shook his head. "I'd planned some moments among the mummies at the museum. I didn't mean to alliterate," he added in surprise.

"You probably made it up on your way over. Anyway, if it's too nice a day for movies, it's too nice for mummies."

Wally disagreed. He thought there was something particularly right in stepping from the sun of a young spring day into the vast shadowed repository of olden things. There was, in the museum, a lintel and passageway taken from a temple built by Ramses II at Thebes, an earthenware hippopotamus with painted lotus flowers beneath the glaze, a green stone head of a cat. The knowledge of once-living hands carving the relief in the narrow passage, painting the lotus that bloomed three thousand years ago, capturing an immobile feline glance from which the light had been gone so many centuries, touched in Wally a chord of awe, a stirring sense of the past forever living. His hand resting on stone that had known the hand of Pharaoh on his way to worship, his eyes appraising the curve and color of a leaf that the eye of Nefertiti had once traced. That this communion with the past was here, accessible, in the present, moved a deep gratitude in Wally. One he could never rightly explain to Gretchen.

"They're so dead," she complained now. When Wally didn't reply, she went on, "I don't mean their civilization. I mean they were dead when they lived. Everything you see or hear about them shows that all they cared about was dying. No wonder their culture decayed . . . it was a necrophile culture."

Ah, thought the pedant Wally, but "Sceptre, learning physik must follow this and come to dust." He always found it difficult adequately to defend his own ideas, because he had a not entirely welcome facility for seeing how reasonably another could disagree. And so few people ever changed their opinions through being argued with. To explain an emotion, the sort he felt in the presence of ancient things, was quite impossible.

"All right," he said, "What would you and Nelle like?"

But they couldn't decide either, so Wally suggested simply driving out in the country.

"We'll drop Mrs. Gibson at her sister's first. All right?" Gretchen asked.

"Anywhere at all," he protested.

"Aren't you a dear?" Mrs. Gibson said, jumping to her feet. "Now if you'll just wait till I get my hat out of the icebox, I'll be with you." She tripped off toward the kitchen.

"What did she say?" Wally asked cautiously

"She has to get her hat," Nelle answered.

"Did . . . out of the icebox?"

41

"That's where Mother keeps them. In the spring and summer Mother always has her hats made by the florist."

Wally, rather sobered by this, waited for the reappearance of Mrs. Gibson, upon which he took her suitcase (secretly examined in every crevice), then frankly studied her headpiece—three pink geraniums, with their musty-smelling velvet leaves, wired to a yard or so of veiling.

"That's awfully pretty. How many days do you get from a hat?" he asked curiously.

"Two, usually. It really depends on the flowers. With geraniums I can count on three days, but violets fold, *simply* fold. . . ."

"Have you tried orchids?"

Mrs. Gibson considered. "Wouldn't that be rather ostentatious?"

Defeated, Wally took the bag, led the way to his convertible. He let Nelle push the button to send the tentlike cover arcing hugely up and back. Gretchen smiled at the streak of giddiness he uncovered in Nelle. Wally's a catalyst, she thought. Only the reaction on me is negative.

The drive through the country proved to be a not leisured progress along a state parkway admirably kept and well traveled. Trees and grass and flowering laurel there were, on either side of a six-lane highway rolling beneath their white-walled tires at fifty miles an hour. Gretchen, accustomed to Wally's conception of seeing the countryside (Central Park or the Henry Hudson Drive), said nothing. She thought without much interest that Wally was as queer as the next one and kinder than most, then leaned her head against the seat and forgot him.

After lunch, whatever the others wanted, she was going to ask to be driven back. If Rosemary had time when she came off duty, they could play some tennis or perhaps just watch Preston and Dr. Whitney who played so much better, if they were on the courts. Gretchen so enjoyed the sight of Dr. Whitney, white tennis sweater brilliant against his dark skin, that she'd have lingered to watch whether they played well or not. And if they weren't, she could wash some things, study, anyway slough this feeling of silliness that the combination of Wally and Mrs. Gibson, nice as they were, had given her.

Wally and Nelle were discussing archaeology. Nelle's voice had the same tone she used when extolling the rugged strength of the Rockies. She was equally familiar with the Rockies and archaeology—that is, knew nothing at all of either, and her conception of geography was more Hallmark than Rand-McNally, but heart and voice she yearned toward the splendid, mysterious distances. For a moment Gretchen tried to feel for the Sphinx of Gizeh what their ardent words must have meant they felt, but it remained for her a picture in the National Geographic.

She thought idly about Rosemary and Nelle, with whom she'd lived so closely for nearly three years. Nelle, in her opinion, was an enthusiast whose lyric devotion to nursing might easily be rerouted, always provided the new route also led away from home. Well, Mrs. Gibson was certainly a featherhead, and a pretty one. A combination chilling enough to a daughter rather plain and studious. Rosemary Joplin was simply an enigma. Lovely, in a small-boned fragile way, with a wispy manner that made you want to shake her.

Yawning, she listened to Wally describe the troubles Amenhotep IV had had with the Amon priests around 1370 B.C. and recalled her own words to Nelle—something about how fine it would have been to live in the Middle Ages. But that was really just talk. Anyway, she didn't go to museums and hang around the armor rooms. She yawned again. She was hungry and bored and had gotten up too early. She fell asleep.

Chapter 5.

BEHIND the hospital, built on the edge of town with provisions for expansion of which the east wing was a beginning, was a stretch of meadowland. Beyond that, the river. From the sun roof and the upper windows, you could see the Palisades rising sheer and high from the water. Flat ferries burdened with bug-sized cars and trucks drew milky trails behind them as they journeyed to and fro. In the summer, white sails slid lightly over the waves, driving sideways in the wakes of larger craft. Now and then some large, gunned, grey destroyer passed somberly. Freighters, plowing low and laden or high and light, moved past to tell of commerce. Winter or summer, the gulls flew widely in wind and sun. Sometimes they rode on bent wings straight toward the hospital but always banked and slid away before reaching it.

On the sun roof, the patients talked to each other about themselves. In beds, wheelchairs, and on foot, they'd come to feel the sunshine and the warm air. And to talk. . . .

"They tell me it's a matter of salt. Doctor says I can lead a perfectly happy life if I just give up salt. But who can lead a happy life without salt?"

44

"Psychosomatic, that's all you hear any more. I tell you the psychosomatic is running away with the medical profession. . . ."

"Dreary, my dear, *simply* dreary. I spent *months* with my feet higher than my head, and what have I got to show for it?"

"No, honestly, you practically have to bring a death certificate before a doctor will see you these days. . . . And as for getting up at *night!* You could get the plumber faster. . . ."

Rosemary put her small medication tray on the parapet, looked for a moment at the stern wall of cliffs on the other side of the river's traffic. The sun was very warm. It glanced and glimmered in the troughs of the waves, on the pluming crests.

The patients sat or lay around now, after lunch, drowzing. In the garden below, Preston trimmed a hedge, the screech of his shears, snap of green twigs, sounding very clear. In the meadow, daisies and buttercups and Queen Anne's lace thrust through the tall wild grass.

"Do you remember a poem about Queen Anne's lace?" Mrs. Parker asked as Rosemary handed her a little glass of ergot.

Surprised, Rosemary nodded. "Yes, it. . . ."

"Oh, I know how it goes. I just wondered." Mrs. Parker turned back to the river.

> Queen Anne, Queen Anne, she washed her lace,
> All on a summer's day. . . .

Rosemary moved on with the white tray of medicine, wondering if Mrs. Parker's remarks meant that she felt better or worse. It was hard to tell. She decided to mention it to Dr. Grafton. On such a day as this, she thought, it would be difficult not to feel a stirring of life within yourself, just as the moist warm earth was stirring, forgetful of last year's flowers.

45

> Queen Anne, Queen Anne's a long time dead,
> She died a summer's day. . . .

Attending the last of her patients, she started for the stairway, then turned and went back to Mrs. Parker, sitting immobile in the wheelchair, her lovely blue robe lustrous in sunlight.

"Mrs. Parker? Is there anything else you'd like? A glass of ginger ale or. . . ." Or what? A baby? She felt a touch of irritation that Mrs. Parker's sorrow would not respond to the offer of ginger ale. No, thank you, there was nothing Mrs. Parker wanted. Rosemary went back to the door.

> But left her lace to whiten
> On each weed-entangled way.

Back on the floor, Rosemary made beds, enjoying the tight pull of the sheets, the precise mitering of corners.

Mrs. Mew was in the labor room with a girl who couldn't have been more than nineteen, dazedly coping with the spears of her first labor pains and getting little comfort from Mrs. Mew, who was, Rosemary thought, an excellent technician. But she lacked something that makes a nurse not a technician. Compassion, was it? Mrs. Mew had never had a child but had, as she assured the students and patients, a perfect understanding of the process. "You just do as I tell you," she now advised the deep-eyed girl, "and let the pain take care of itself."

Hah, said Rosemary silently. And then, there's one pain around here we'd all be glad to take care of.

Unexpectedly, the girl's voice lifted. "Go away," it said. "You go away and leave me alone."

"Don't be ridiculous," Mrs. Mew blustered. "I'm here to help you."

"Well, you don't help." But the girl's voice trembled, her little show of spirit trickled away. Rosemary wished she could go

46

in there, but of course it was impossibl g as Mew was on hand. She was relieved now to see ultz, the girl's physician, coming through the glass d . Schultz looked like an egg with legs, but he had a m uiling voice, a smooth way of moving that soothed the ightened women.

"Well, Sally," he said to ung patient. "I saw your husband downstairs just no wants to come up, so I said I'd ask how you felt about

Rosemary could feel es of Mrs. Mew's disapproval wash tidally out of the room. She wouldn't, naturally, say a thing to Schultz meone would pay for this sentimentality. Rosemary lad to find it was almost three o'clock, when she ar both went off. Sally would fare better with Mrs. Bra he next shift. Mrs. Brauer thought the new rule of allo sbands to stay a while in the labor room was a very g e. Dr. Schultz had inaugurated it practically single-hand it was all very hard on Mrs. Mew, who had to respec hultz, (wasn't he one of the richest obstetricians in to d at the same time defer to his ideas.

Rosemary snort ew's voice anxiously explaining that "the little lady ha n quite as good as we might wish, doctor, and perhaps i be better if her husband didn't. . . ."

"Nonsense," ultz cut in. "If Sally thinks it would help, we'll have in two shakes."

Sally thought d help.

Mrs. Mew the phone, outraged principles visibly fluttering, to su he husband. Then she whirled on Rosemary, informed a severe tone which intimated that the change was a pi ckery of which the source was obvious, that she was beir erred to evenings on Men's Surgical.

"Though wha ink I'm going to do here with a couple of first-year stud a half-witted graduate who's always stewing about he ife, I don't know." Mrs. Mew glared at Rosemary, defying he...member that the case load was lighter than it had been in ...r that Mrs. Ferris, the graduate, was far from half-witte...possibly entitled to worry about her sick husband and ch...me trying to take care of each other.

All Rosemary said was, "Thank...rs. Mew," and, professionally, they parted forever, tho...y would meet from time to time in the halls of the Reside...ere Mrs. Mew remained year after year. The students...ht it was pretty grim. Each one assured herself that, n...r what the rest did, she would never be thirty, good heav...l still washing in a community bathroom, eating in a com...dining room, recreating in a community recreation room...couldn't, in a sense, really part from Mrs. Mew. Rosema...ted whether anyone who worked with her could actually...it. As Gretchen said, she was the best horrible example...ospital and would probably, in years to come, account for...kindness in nurses trying not to be like her.

From her room in the Residence at a little ...ee, Rosemary glanced over at the sun roof, looking for ...rker. She spied the gleaming blue robe. Beside Mrs. ...chair, a long figure lounged against the parapet. Even ...unlight hadn't flashed on the Kelly clamp, Rosemary wou...known it was Dr. Grafton. The two seemed deep in con...l, Mrs. Parker quite as active as the doctor. Rosemary ...as she moved away from the window. Nelle was right. ...'s some doctor.

She stretched, pulled the spread to the foot ...ed, and lay down, luxuriating in the soft support of the ... There was one thing to be said for the Residence; its ...ses were marvelous. Two things, really. The other that...e of the irregular hours of training, they simply had to ...a room of your own. The door could be shut, the transom closed, and there you were. Free to add to your always depleted store of sleep, to read, write, dream, unwatched and unquestioned. For the students, even the ones who'd had rooms of their own at home, the Residence with all its laws about hours represented more freedom than most of them had ever known. During the first year especially, there was an exultant sensation of liberty, exempt from the family eyes, the family presence. Gretchen said that, after she'd been accepted in the school, one of the first things she'd thought was how perfectly super it would be not to help with the cooking—not even to know what you were going to have till you sat down. Of course now, in her third year, this element of enthusiasm had disappeared entirely. For three years, except for vacations or the nights they ate out (Gretchen, in this respect, was better off than anyone else), they'd been eating what appeared to be tastily prepared leftovers. Who got whatever it had been on the first night was a question, but they gloomily supposed that what was hash to them had been a roast in the doctors' dining room twenty-four hours earlier. Rebellions were mostly sub rosa, except for the time Gretchen had stormed up to the counter with a dish of wobbly custard described on the menu as floating island.

"Will you tell me what's floating about this island?" she demanded, poking it at a weary server.

The girl looked at Gretchen, at the custard, took a spoonful of jam and dropped it with a jerk that sent it plunging through the quivering yellow surface. "Jam is," she said, in a tone that convinced even the intrepid Gretchen that the issue of floating island was closed. For the most part, they ate what they got, took out their cravings in chocolate bars and dreams.

Against her judgment, Rosemary closed her eyes, knowing the assurance she gave herself that she'd get up in a minute was nonsense.

This really was the most wonderful mattress. . . .

49

Nurses sleep at any opportunity, and Rosemary would have slept now but for the voices of two people waiting for the elevator which came clearly through the transom. Not familiar voices, so they must be freshmen. She caught her own name, thought of calling out that they should speak well of her, but languor lay on her tongue as well as her body, and she said nothing.

"Well, which ever one I'd want to be like, it won't be Joplin," one of the voices was saying.

Oh gosh, thought Rosemary, do I really have to put up with this? And she said nothing.

"She's the sort of person who's a great help in time of trouble. My mother says they're on your step with hot soup before the body is cold, and after a while trouble is all you connect them with."

"Oh, that isn't fair. She's awfully good to the patients. Everyone says so."

"She's too good. I mean, all those sympathetic glances and things. If I were sick, it would drive me crazy to have a nurse so . . . so commiserating. She'd make you think you were dying if you had a broken thumb."

"Better than the ones who are so darned cheerful."

Their conversation was swallowed in the arrival and departure of the elevator.

Without noticing, Rosemary had gotten up and now found herself looking angrily in the mirror. "I am *not*," she said aloud, and then glanced toward the transom. But I'm not, she went on to herself. The girl in the mirror glared at her, and she couldn't help noticing that the flushed cheeks were becoming. I ought to get a sunburn, she decided, opening the closet door. She pulled out a plaid skirt, white sweater, socks, and loafers. I don't like jolly nurses, she told herself impatiently. If I were sick, I wouldn't want someone cantering around me with a cheery smile. Well, now, don't we look *fine* today! She knotted a blue scarf at her throat, brushed her blonde hair till it crackled. Still, she thought, resting the brush against her hand, still, perhaps other people would like it. Gretchen says a hospital is a place to get well in. I must learn to think that way, too.

She took the elevator downstairs, walked without much aim along the path bordered with just-budding iris. Gretchen, she went on in her thoughts, is a good nurse. Not gay, but not *too* kind. An air of "Well, this isn't too pleasant, but we'll get it over with and then you'll feel better." That sort of nurse. She wondered now where Gretchen was. Out probably, with Wally or one of her less frequently seen men. Gretchen really had the most amazing facility for finding men no matter where she went. Or not really finding them because she didn't hunt. Merely by being someplace, she caused men to appear.

Was it coincidence that she stopped then at the sound of music coming softly through an open ground-floor window? That she leaned against a scaling ivory-grey beech tree, closing her eyes to hear the music?

"Like it?" asked a voice she recognized without opening her eyes.

"Oh, very much," she said, opening them then to look at Dr. Grafton, who leaned on the window sill, his starched white sleeves pushing against the screen. He shoved the screen up to lean out further.

"Is this your room?" she asked, glancing past him into the small neat room where a radiophonograph stood among the hospital furnishings. He nodded, and they both fell silent while the music, Brahm's *Alto Rhapsody*, twined round the richness of Marion Anderson's great voice. He had the volume turned low, so the melancholy beauty of the horns, the strings, the deeply tender voice, were lost a little. But still the splendid unfolding of orchestra, chorus, and that one divine voice held them unspeaking to the last lingering fall of the music, motionless for a moment after.

Dr. Grafton turned into his room to remove the records. He came back to the window. "I'm glad you happened by. I like to share music. I'd have played it louder, only it doesn't seem very considerate."

Rosemary sighed, the spell still on her. "I should think anyone would love to hear it."

"Well, it doesn't work out that way. Mrs. Smith is sure to say Brahms is a bust but how about boogie, and Mr. Jones will complain to the director that he came here to be cured, not concussed, and for every one patient who liked it, I'd have sixteen ready to rip the phonograph apart. I keep it low in order to keep it at all."

"How did you get along with Mrs. Parker?" Rosemary asked abruptly.

Dr. Grafton looked at her with interest. "I got her talking," he said tentatively.

"Well, that's progress, with Mrs. Parker."

"Are you interested in her case?"

Rosemary, remembering her decision of a few minutes ago, said, "Not particularly." At his expression, she added, "At least, not any more. I mean, I've decided not to be particularly interested in any of the patients from now on."

"Why is that?"

Rosemary pushed her hair back. "Oh, it's all terribly long and involved and wouldn't make sense probably anyway." He still regarded her inquiringly, so she plodded on. "I've discovered that I'm the sort of nurse who hovers about with the solicitude which kills. So—I'm going to try to get over it."

"You think you can?"

"I can try."

"Who says you're too solicitous?"

"Oh, people. . . ."

"It's possible," he said consideringly. "A thing like that could

52

happen, but I'm inclined to feel the patients would mind it a good deal less than some—'people'—may think." He spoke as though his attention was completely on the question of Rosemary's professional relationships. He'll be one of those people, she thought, who's interested in everybody. It made her rather irritable. She didn't care for people who spread themselves so thin with everyone they couldn't get thick with anyone. Only it was, she decided, rather a good description of herself. Her eyes moved from an intense regard of her own feet to his face. Such a young, wise, nice face. A speculative face.

He said he and Mrs. Parker had just discussed aimless things today.

"I think it's marvelous she discussed anything at all. But she did say something about sea gulls to me this morning, about how they never seem to die while anyone's looking. It wasn't that exactly. . . ."

"I know. She mentioned it to me too. Her husband's going to bring her some field glasses, so she can study them when she's on the roof."

"Maybe if she watches them flying, she'll forget about them dying."

"I hoped so." Dr. Grafton seemed more and more pleased with their conversation, and Rosemary had, for the first time in her life, the delight of knowing, without preliminaries, that she'd made a friend. Unaware of it herself, Rosmary had the kind of snobbery which prevented her from speaking of anything she considered worth while to anyone she didn't know very well. Even her kindness to invalids was based on the unconscious assumption that she could be interested in them, but they could not be in her. Since friendship does not consist merely of being a good listener, she had few friends. Gretchen and Nelle came as close as anyone ever had, and there were, among the three of them, all sorts of reservations. She had sometimes thought Preston, to whom she spoke more easily than to anyone else, could be her friend. But Preston had a quality of disinterested interest that discouraged close relationships. Like a philosopher, she thought. You could discuss almost anything with a philosopher, but you couldn't feel much with him.

Dr. Grafton leaned even further out his window, as though to close up the distance between them. His Kelly clamp caught on the screen hook, pulled from his pocket, fell to the grass beneath his window before he could retrieve it. Rosemary picked it up, held the shiny instrument a moment before handing it back. Then, rather dismayed at her own audacity, she said, "Why do you wear it?"

He looked surprised, tapping the clamp with his finger, his eyes on her. "We all. . . . Does it look silly?"

"Oh, no," she said quickly. "Just . . . sort of young."

He shook his head. "Well, that won't do at all." Seeming to realize that she'd made herself nervous, he added, "Thanks. That was very thoughtful of you." But he made no explanation, and obscurely that comforted Rosemary, who wanted to feel that he was sure of himself.

Now, she thought, there is really nothing left except to leave. Since he hadn't asked her name and apart from Mrs. Parker, a subject not inexhaustible, she could think of nothing further to say, her pride, compromised by each passing moment of silence, demanded that she remove herself. Please, she thought, make him ask my name. And then in a sudden fluster, with a mere wave of the hand, she started away.

"Oh, say," he called after her, "I forgot to ask your name."

Chapter 6.

GRETCHEN was put on Pediatrics, eleven at night to seven in the morning, Nelle and Rosemary on the private wing of Men's Surgery, three in the afternoon to eleven at night. It would be their last change before graduation, and the only one who was pleased was Gretchen.

Rosemary, despite the handicap of Mrs. Mew, had liked O.B. Now, in addition, she admitted to a disappointment in being put on Surgery, because Dr. Grafton was a medical intern, so she'd probably only see him in the halls, if then. Nelle didn't like the hours. She had also some formless objection to the private wings, based in part on the presence of so many specials, the type of nurse for whom Nelle felt a deep, quite unexplained, antipathy.

They had all been on these floors before. Their presence now was not in the way of clinical experience but hospital necessity. Their's was a practically graduate status; courses of instruction had been discontinued; and in all but the financial sense they were on as staff nurses to fill gaps.

Gretchen was delighted with her change. She'd been in the Operating Room, where she was rated one of the best surgical nurses they had. She liked its excitement, its precision, its drama. The great glass ceiling, gleaming Mayo trays, slap of instruments in the surgeons' gloved hands, low knowledgeable voices, anesthetist looking rather like a pilot at his great machine. But she missed people. The only time she saw the patients was when she went down with an orderly and a padded stretcher to bring them up to the operating room. By then, they were usually drugged almost to the point of sleep, and they certainly never recalled her later. Being put on Pediatrics was fine, for Gretchen felt very comfortable with children. In fact, she adored them, though it was not generally known, for wouldn't it be a bit absurd to go about saying she loved children, as though it were a virtue, as though some special benefit should accrue as a result? Always impatient with people who announced their affections proudly (they loved oatmeal, flowers, Puccini—the object of their love not so important as the fact of it), Gretchen rarely claimed even to care for something. It sounded too like boasting. It was, of course, all right for Dr. Bradley to say children were the most important people on earth. She'd been selling something and was in a position to praise it. What she said was obvious, but since the obvious isn't always apparent, it was as well that people like Dr. Bradley were around to point it out. For the rest of us, Gretchen thought, a little reserve is a good thing.

The morning of the day she went on Pediatrics, Gretchen slept late. She missed breakfast, very nearly missed lunch. Then, with a self-conscious eye on the beautiful day, she returned to the fourth floor to make herself some chocolate fudge in the little kitchen. There was no reason to think that this time, any more than in times past, the fudge would harden properly, but there was always a spoon, and fudge she must have.

"Really," she said to Rosemary who'd been lured in by the fragrance wafted through the halls, "Really, they don't give us enough sweet stuff. The human system simply can't do without sweets; you'd think the dieticians would know that."

"Do you really think about food as much as you seem to?"

What a forthright person she is, Gretchen thought. She was two years older than Rosemary, but more than that lay behind Gretchen's feeling that dealing with Rosemary was very like dealing with her own little sister Prudence. Thinking of Prudence, a sudden current of delight seized Gretchen. Pretty soon now, she could go home. Summer at home. The thought was intoxicating in a way that would have astounded the Gretchen of three years ago. A summer in the small balsam-ringed cottage by the Indiana lake she'd been so bored with three years ago. It seemed now the only desirable thing in life, to have all her sprawling, exigent, glancing, argumentative family around her again. Prudence, sixteen, half-enchanted, half-defiant. William, nineteen, wonderfully joyous uncomplicated boy. Hally, a sober fourteen, whose once-annoying resistance to frivolity now seemed only restful. And Noah, an eight-year-old example of the theory of dynamism. Impossible now that she'd ever wished to leave them, that her mother had ever seemed too managing, her father too lazy, the children too much with her. I want to go home, she thought. I'm simply dying to go home. It was a wonderful wish because it wouldn't be denied her. For Gretchen, quite as uncomplicated a person as her brother William, realization was much better than anticipation.

"Not really," she answered Rosemary's question, "only griping about it is the one privilege attached to institutional food. I like to employ my privileges." She stirred vigorously, tired of it, removed the pot and dropped a large pat of butter in the dark bubbling lava. "Do you think this would harden if I put it away and didn't look for a few days?"

"I suppose anything will harden if it's left alone long enough."

Gretchen looked closely at the oval, lovely face before her but found nothing there to picture the thoughts which lay behind.

She stirred the fudge, beat it, and waited hopefully for a sign of thickening. She'd been thinking of something, something very nice. . . . Oh yes, home. Pretty soon now. And meanwhile, it would be fine if this stuff would act like fudge.

"They're planning a graduation ball," Rosemary said.

"When?"

"A week from Saturday. Dorry Palmer is collecting a dollar from everybody for decorations. I hope she thinks of something besides Japanese lanterns."

"If she can't, there's no point in taking our dollars. There must be enough Japanese lanterns left around from her other dances that would do very nicely if someone would sew them up and blow the dust off."

"We should get a new decorations committee or anyway new decorations. Maybe the dollars are for refreshments."

"I think they save those from one dance to the next, too."

"Why don't you make them some fudge?"

"Careful what you're saying, or I won't give you a piece of this."

"You mean a spoonful," Rosemary reminded her.

Gretchen poured her mixture in a pan, set it aside. "How's your new doctor?" she inquired as they went down the hall to Rosemary's room.

But Rosemary became evasive. "Will you go with Wally?" she asked, getting a uniform.

"To the dance? Maybe not. I think perhaps he and Nelle might go. They could discuss the rise of Alexander as they waltzed. I never can keep up with Wally's conversations."

"Don't you care? If he takes Nelle, I mean?"

Gretchen turned her head a little but had the grace not to

smile. "Oh, no. I think it would be nice. Would you like me to get you an import? I mean, I know you can get your own, but I just thought. ..."

She knows nothing of the sort, Rosemary thought. She buttoned the starchy white bib, shoved scissors in the huge patch pocket. But how could you get annoyed with Gretchen? Her generosity was so slap-dash, so completely without hauteur or pride. She offered her men as she'd offer a handkerchief, if she had lots and you had none, with the same assumption that the situation was, of course, temporary. Still, Rosemary wasn't having any this time. No one cared much for the dances. Extra men, "imports," were hard to find. The interns didn't have time for dances, the residents didn't have time for nurses, the nurses were usually too tired to dance.

"I have to run," Rosemary said, bobby-pinning her flaring student cap.

"I'll walk over with you."

As they went along the path to the hospital, Nelle hurried up beside them. "Where are you off to?" she said to Gretchen.

"Take a walk, I guess."

"You're lucky. Darn these private wings anyway."

Gretchen smiled. "What's the matter, Nelle? Do you think everyone should be in a ward even if he has money to moan in private?"

"Gosh, no. It's the specials—they kill me. Act like princesses among the peasants."

"Oh, for heaven's sake, Nelle, you'd think you'd found another species. They're people, you know."

Nelle jerked her shoulders, not answering.

The flaunting sharp red bricks of the new wing were strident beside the larger mellow bulk of the old hospital. Along the walls, rambler roses were pinkly profuse. In border gardens the iris, cousin to the orchid, budded toward blooming. Beyond

59

the tennis courts, Preston, in faded tight dungarees, was climbing a ladder laid against a maple.

"There certainly is something about jeans," Gretchen mused, watching him.

"You mean something about pants, don't you?" Nelle snapped, then flushed at Gretchen's laugh. "Sorry, I'm just in a bad mood."

"Well, you're entitled to be once in a while," Gretchen assured her. Again Nelle wouldn't reply. She reached the floor in a sullen mood, and Rosemary was glad to part company when Mrs. Peder assigned their duties.

An hour later, Nelle, changing a dressing in a semiprivate room, saw her patient start suddenly.

"Where do you suppose she's going with that screen?" he muttered.

Nelle turned in time to see one of the specials in question disappear through the door with the only folding screen in the room. It was used between the beds for doctors' consultations, for privacy when either of the men wished it, and had been leaning against the wall when the special entered, not knocking, and walked off with it, not speaking. An unaccustomed anger rose in Nelle and, for once, was not immediately banished. But she said calmly enough, "I'll try to get it back."

"Nervy woman," the patient snapped. "Not a by-your-leave or anything."

"Mmm," said Nelle, annoyed, but not enough to enter a joint assault against another nurse. She finished the dressing, took herself down the corridor, poking her head in each room. Arrived at 426, she found the nurse busily arranging her pilfered screen as a buffer against drafts.

"I'd like to have that screen back, please," Nelle said, low so as not to disturb the patient, but with enough intensity to startle the special, who gripped the screen tightly.

"Kindly explain what you're doing," the nurse said, moving toward the door. "Coming in here without knocking. . . ."

"You," Nelle said firmly, aware of surprise at her own voice which ordinarily trembled at the mention of a scene, "walked in there without knocking. That's the only screen they have."

"I need a screen in here, and there wasn't any." The special turned away, secure in her position as graduate talking to student. She implied the interview was at an end.

"I'm sorry," Nelle said, "but I'm going to take it back."

The special turned, surprise in every feature. "When I was a student," she said thinly, "We didn't dare speak this way to graduate nurses. . . ."

"Perhaps the graduates in your day were more helpful. If you won't let me take this screen back, please do it yourself."

"I can't leave my patient. And you're bothering him. And me."

"You left your patient long enough to take the screen, didn't you?"

Suddenly overwhelmed, the special pushed past her. "I'm going to report you. Right now."

Nelle hesitated, slightly alarmed but still angry enough not to care. She grabbed the screen, smiled quickly at the man in bed, who stared in astonishment, started back down the hall.

"Miss Gibson. Oh, Miss Gibson!" The head nurse almost ran to catch up with her. "What are you thinking of? Miss O'Donnell says you've taken her screen. What in the world is this?" Mrs. Peder, completely bewildered, went so far as to scratch her head.

"*She* took it," Nelle glared. "She just walked into 410 and took it. Those men need their screen to begin with, and to go on with. . . ."

"Just a second," said the flustered Mrs. Peder, who couldn't comprehend such an outburst from nice calm Miss Gibson.

She patted the air, almost as if she patted Nelle. "Now, let's get this straight. Miss O'Donnell, did you take the screen or did Miss Gibson?"

"She did," they said together.

"Oh, this is ridiculous. You'll both come with me to the desk. Miss Merkle is the one to attend to this."

"I can't leave my patient," Miss O'Donnell said again.

Mrs. Peder flicked her an irritable glance. "You've already left him. Anyway, he hasn't gone up yet. He'll keep for a minute or so."

"I don't propose to put up with this," Miss O'Donnell said, biting her lip, "I'll find a screen somewhere else."

"You mean you did take it?"

Miss O'Donnell sighed angrily. "If the hospital doesn't provide screens in its private rooms, then it's up to the nurse to find one."

"It isn't up to her to take one from somebody else," Mrs. Peder said icily. "You may come to the desk with such requests. Go along, Miss Gibson." She turned back to the special. "I'll ring for a porter, and a screen will be sent up. That's all."

Mrs. Peder went to the desk. Miss O'Donnell flounced, there was no other word for it, into 426. And Nelle rather swaggered back to 410 where she received an uproarious greeting.

The incident bucked her up for the rest of the day. Obviously, it was silly to dislike the private wings. Quite suddenly, she wished that Wally could have seen her, defending her screen, or shield, you might say. Defending her unequal position with a spirit so unlike her. In the normal course of things, Nelle, faced with a scene, would pacify or flee, whichever was simpler. But here she had actually sailed into enemy territory and emerged triumphant. The results were marvelously bracing. So bracing that if she weren't careful, the thought occurred with a smile, it could become a habit. And an habitually spirited defense of one's rights would probably amount just to bad temper. The idea of having a temper to curb so amused Nelle that she laughed aloud.

"What the devil do you find so funny?" snapped the patient she'd just speared with a penicillin hypo.

"I'm sorry," said Nelle, unable not to smile.

The man eyed her with cold dislike. "Nothing like a hearty laugh for a sick man, is there?" he said maliciously. Abruptly tears spilled on his cheeks. He waited a moment to be sure she'd notice, then turned weakly away.

"I am sorry," Nelle repeated with distaste. This man, this sort of man, was familiar now after three years of every known type of patient. He was wringing each drop of emotion from his status as an invalid. Not only prepared, but insistent upon, dying a thousand deaths (though with no intention at all of dying a single one), he would drain the sympathetic resources of a saint. His family, conceivably not saints, would be crushed between the millstones of their natural pity and his demands for yet more. Nelle wished she could jab him again, but an even subtler thrust was possible.

She waited till he turned toward her again, gave him a bright broad smile, an energetic nod. "You're looking *fine*," she said intensely. "Just absolutely *fine*. . . ." Another smile for his out-raged stare, and she skipped off.

My, she thought, I am in a horrible mood today. I really should try it oftener. She recalled with a start her nasty but quite unpremeditated remark to Gretchen. It would be rather disagreeable if having a temper (and could you get a temper all of a sudden?) meant snarling at your friends. Of course, Gretchen would make it worse by not taking offense. She wondered what it would be like to be so sure, within yourself, that you could shrug away barbs like that. It wasn't an attitude that could be assumed. If the barb hit, no matter how you shrugged, your face would burn, your voice shake, something would give you away. I wouldn't want to be so insensitive, she told herself, and immediately, yes, I would. I'd love it. To be insensitive Gretchen's way, not because you were dull but because you were so irreducibly bright, would be heaven. She sighed, less pert now. Wally, though he didn't act it, was probably terribly in love with Gretchen. Most of the men who trailed around after her were.

She passed Miss O'Donnell in the hall, glad that Wally couldn't see her now, averting her eyes from the level gaze of her defeated enemy.

"Miss Joplin, will you attend to Mr. Chalmers and Mr. Rose? That's 460." Mrs. Peder looked from her charting at Rosemary. "Seconal for both of them, codeine for Rose. Check the sheet first."

Mrs. Peder looked tired. Rosemary, blinking a little, was pretty sure she did too. It was hard at first, getting used to new hours. She looked at the medication sheet, drew the little white tray forward. Almost ten o'clock. The last of the visitors were moving down the hall, talking in low tones. Nighttime silence, with its undercurrents of motion and sound, was settling on the darkened corridors. Outside closed doors, vases of flowers, gay or drooping, stood like tiny brilliant sentinels. Like little toy soldiers, Rosemary thought, wondering why the poetry she remembered from childhood was always the sad poetry. Oh, the terrible sadness of Little Boy Blue. *The years are many, the years are long....*

"If I ever have any children, I'll see to it that they don't read Little Boy Blue," Rosemary said to Mrs. Peder.

"What? Oh, I'm sure you will, a pretty girl like you," Mrs. Peder assured her absently.

Rosemary, walking down the hall, aware of the silent tread of her rubber soles, aware of the dark hours ahead crouching like soft cats in corners, aware of sleeplessness beginning its show of strength, drew a deep breath and wondered if she'd be sitting, like Mrs. Peder, through the years to come, at a charting desk, tired in the night. She wondered why Mrs. Peder, who had two little boys, worked these hours. Only one night a week to bathe those bouncy boys' bodies herself, one night to read a drowzy story, to open a window and firmly tuck the healthy rebels against sleep into their own low beds. She must miss them terribly. But for some reason Rosemary couldn't know or ask, there she was, working away the sweetest hours of her children's lives.

Will I be like that? Rosemary wondered. Or perhaps she wouldn't be married at all. Would she then, be like Miss Merkle? She made a picture for herself of Miss Merkle and Dollar, now, at almost ten o'clock P.M. The scanty dishes for one washed and put away. The small apartment neatly ordered and silent. Did they sit together companionably, Miss Merkle's square hands reaching down now and then to scratch a draggly ear, cup the round head in a slow massage, making up for the hours he spent alone? Miss Merkle reading a novel, sewing perhaps? Dollar lying on his side, breathing heavily, wagging in this evening security the tail that had never been seen to wag at the hospital? Was that a picture of Miss Merkle tonight? Was it, possibly, a picture of Rosemary twenty years from to-night?

"Have you ever noticed that pathologist, Dr. Prosser?" Gretchen had asked one day.

Rosemary had remembered him but nothing about him.

"Well, he's the sort of doctor who only likes parts of patients. He's so cemented to the tissue in question that he never notices a person goes with it. I think," said Gretchen, sounding arch in

65

order not to sound solemn, "that it's awfully easy to fall in the way of fixing your eyes on such a little part of life that you forget all about living. I'm apt to get thinking it's all fun. And some people," she had gone on, without apparent purpose, "some people get to brooding on its grey spots, don't you think?"

Rosemary, quite aware of the purpose behind Gretchen's little homily, had even been grateful for it. But the hardest profit in the world to take is profit from good advice, and here she was, still forever chasing grey spots.

She knocked gently on the door of 460, entered to find one patient's chair drawn up beside the other's bed. The two men were talking earnestly, broke off midsentence as she slipped in.

"Evening, nurse," said the man in the chair. The patient in bed nodded. Rosemary recognized him as the operative case who'd been discussing Snead's putting as he went off to meet the surgeon's knife.

"Are you Mr. Rose?" she asked him.

"Right. How'd you know?"

"I guessed. There's a fifty-per-cent chance of being right in a semiprivate, so I always try." The two men laughed, but an air of unfinished words hung over them as they took their medicine.

"I'll straighten the beds and be gone in a minute," she assured them, moving first toward Mr. Chalmers' empty one.

Politely relieved, they turned toward each other. Mr. Chalmers drummed thoughtfully on the chair arm, then recollected at what point he'd been interrupted.

"Oh yes, yes. Well, he drove it a clean hundred seventy-five yards, and it went on the green like a pin to a magnet. Six inches from the cup. Didn't say a word, you know. Just stepped back. Smiling. And do you think *I* get on the green? Me, who's made a birdie on that hole more times than I can count? Like hell I do. Right into the trap. *Right into it!*" He sank back in his chair with a gusty sigh. Mr. Rose shook his head, wordless.

66

"You couldn't," Mr. Chalmers said moodily after a short silence, "You couldn't get out of that trap with a steam shovel."

"What'd you make on the hole?" Mr. Rose asked in a kindly tone.

"Seven."

"What's par?" Mr. Rose couldn't have been gentler if he'd been a doctor himself, soliciting delicate but vital information.

"Four."

There was silence, during which Rosemary turned her back to them and tried not to laugh.

"You'd better come to bed now, Mr. Chalmers," she said, giving the pillow a brisk pat. She moved over to attend to Mr. Rose, who was pleasant but inattentive. "You know," he said at length, to his now recumbant roommate, "I'm getting a special bulletin, gives me the probable weather for a few months ahead. Doctor tells me I'll be able to play nine holes round about the end of July, so I've been studying it up. About decided to go to Pennsylvania for a few weeks. Less rain, from the looks of it."

"That right?" Mr. Chalmers said quizzically. "You usually play around here?"

"Oh sure. I always figure if there's a good course close to home, why go away for vacations? But this isn't any ordinary year. I'll be missing a clear three months. So if my bulletin's right, and it ought to be, Pennsylvania's the best bet." He nodded soberly, picture of a man not given to hasty decisions arriving at a considered one.

Mr. Chalmers was looking impressed and thoughtful as Rosemary bid them good night.

And that, she thought, is another example of concentrating all your vision on a little piece of life. Only what a lot of fun they got out of their piece. She hoped their wives did too.

In her room, when she got there at a bit past eleven, were a few proudly square pieces of fudge resting on a note from

Gretchen. "Do you suppose this is the real thing?" Gretchen's lazy hand demanded, "or is it just a flash in the pan?"

At a quarter to eleven, Gretchen also put three pieces of fudge in Nelle's room, without a note, stuffed six more in a paper bag for herself, started toward the hospital. The night was warm, moonless, starless. The mothy, honeysuckled dark was almost a substance, something you could hold in your hand, if you turned your fingers lightly.

On Pediatrics, it sifted through screened windows but lost itself then in the heavy iodoformed air.

"You'll be on alone tonight, Miss Bemis," the tired floor nurse said when they'd gone over the charts. She rose, rubbed her forehead with a stubby hand, half-smiled, but found the effort too great. "I'm sure you'll be all right, and if anything does come up, you can phone the office."

Gretchen didn't protest. She'd never had sole charge of a floor before, but if she couldn't handle it now, then there were three years of training gone for nothing.

She moved quickly through the darkened ward, pausing at each barred bed to eye the little occupant. Most of them slept the pliant curled sleep of little things, animals or children. Here and there a child with flowery breath that well children seem always to have. But from most of the parted lips a feverish soft surging, broken now and then with a sigh.

She changed a sobbing baby's diapers, then held him a while, pushing back the damp curls when he lifted his heavy head. Then when it fell again to her shoulder, patting his back gently. She sang softly in the undramatic monotone so lovely for lullabies, idle little words of her own,

"Sleep well, my little rosy baby, sleep until the night is gone,
Sleep now my cozy rosy baby, you're sure to be awake by dawn,
Dream well, da dum de dum. . . ."

After a bit, she eased him into his crib, and with the comfort of a thumb in his mouth he slept lightly.

From then till three she had no time for the fudge or for the book she'd optimistically taken along. Gretchen always took a book on night duty but never had a chance to read. Tonight, with no help at all, with seven patients to watch, three formulas to give, several one-o'clock medications, charts to be written up, she didn't have a moment to remember the novel and the candy shoved in a desk drawer.

At three o'clock, a half-hour's relief.

In the dining room, she selected food at random, never quite sure whether she was eating lunch or dinner at this hour, sat with a heavy sigh at a table by the window. The first few nights really were hard. After that, you got used to it, got so you cherished the oddly valuable hours usually lost. Reasonable or not, if you waked and worked while others slept, you were for that time superior. Aware of your height, your thinking, your hands moving. Aware of the sleeping around you. Only, tonight, her pleasure in wakefulness was slender. She'd have happily been inferior to be also asleep. She concentrated on her watch, decided there was time for one more cup of coffee.

The ward, at four-thirty, was comparatively quiet, with patients sleeping heavily. Gretchen was at the window, watching the lights of river traffic, thinking how now, though it was still dark, anyone would know morning wasn't far. The birds knew. A clear questioning note would come like a reed through the silence now and then.

The low buzz of the phone brought her hurrying to the desk. "Patient of Dr. Whitney's coming up," the office voice informed, "Temperature 105. Standing orders till the doctor gets here. Name, Donal Banning, age five. Probably rheumatic fever. Everything all right up there, Miss Bemis?"

"Everything's fine."

Gretchen hung up, went to one of the glass cubicles to prepare a bed for the patient, who arrived in a few minutes on a stretcher. A handsome, flushed boy, obviously robust, only now very ill. He turned his bullet head with its thick yellow hair from side to side, muttering little mashed phrases of no sense. The orderly, with automatic tenderness, transferred him from stretcher to bed, but even at that delicate touch he cried out in protest. When the doctor arrived, tall, wide awake, with an early-morning freshness about his clothes, the patient had fallen into a half slumber. Dr. Whitney's examination and orders were quick and brusque. He stood for a moment after the medication was given watching the tousled tense sleeper with brooding eyes.

"It's . . . tough," he said finally, inadequately, and turned away.

Gretchen walked beside him without words. Then, at the door of the diet kitchen, on an impulse hardly explicable, she asked whether he'd like a cup of coffee. They looked at each other in surprise, the offer being analagous to a palace guard inviting the King to share a spot of tea. But he nodded and followed her into the kitchen.

As Gretchen heated the little pot in which she'd made coffee earlier, Dr. Whitney walked to the window. Night was a lingering grey guest soon to be sped. On river and meadows mist moved and spun slowly, a low white sea. Birds sang in a wild spangled harmony and burst from tree and thicket, enraptured with the dawn.

Dr. Whitney thrust his nose toward the screen, breathing deeply. "Always new, isn't it?" he said, turning for his coffee, then sitting on the sill to drink it. "This is good of you."

Gretchen, abruptly overcome with awe at his presence, managed a smile, sipped at her coffee, and wished she could think of a comment. Having never experienced shyness before, she felt uncertain how to deal with it, and a little entranced at having to deal with it at all. So many stories that were told of Dr. Whitney

70

now tumbled in her mind as she stood with him here in the kitchen. Stories of his skill, his silent patience with errors (more unnerving than the loud scorn of, say, Dr. Alvord), his unsociability masked by the most scrupulous courtesy, the incredibly long hours he worked without tiring. The stories recalled, and his large very handsome presence, the unassuming strength in his eyes, his voice, combined to make Gretchen, for the first time that she could recall, feel hesitant and quite inadequate to any reply, no matter how simple seeming.

Dr. Whitney, who was rather tired and had in his ears the echo of a day's conversation, the sort of conversation a doctor hears on a busy day, found Gretchen's silence, the hot coffee, the rose and blue vaporing dawn, all very peaceful. Gradually, he found himself talking. First of Donal Banning, a wonderful bloom from a seedy family. Then of rheumatic fever. And then—of himself.

"I'd planned to do heart research. Funny, how you think your future will always be there. I suppose doctors are apt to because it takes so long to get started. . . . You think your future is ahead, so it won't matter at all if you just practice a little, work with another doctor for a while. Marvelous experience and all. Then, the first thing you know. . . ." He put aside his empty cup but made no move to leave. "There you are, big practice . . . no research. And it isn't what you meant at all." After a pause, "I meant to be the one who tried to prevent Donal Banning from coming here tonight with acute rheumatic fever, not the one who diagnosed it."

Gretchen was silent. For what could she have said? He was talking but not inviting solutions. Breathlessly privileged to listen, she waited, very still, hoping that for a little while there would be no cry from the ward.

"You see," Dr. Whitney explained (in order to make things clear to whom?), "when I went in with Gardner Wylie, I

71

thought that with his big cardiac practice I'd get a lot of good experience. Neither one of us thought I'd be there long. Just till the men in the Army got back and could ease the strain on him. Good for both of us, we thought." He shook his head, sadly, a little wearily now, "Poor Gardner...," and got up from the window sill. An apricot morning spread gently from the West over meadows and river. It turned the hard cliffs of the Palisades to pleats of softness. Fewer birds sang. But in the ward, children stirred.

Dr. Whitney went in to glance at Donal Banning once more, returned quickly. "Thanks for the coffee, Miss Bemis." He seemed to pull himself out of a reverie, to become again the abstractly courteous Dr. Whitney one encountered in the corridors. Dr. Whitney, highly respected, rarely addressed but in a professional capacity. With a nod, a brief smile, he strode away to begin his day's work, having concluded his night's work. He was whistling softly as he turned the corner.

It's no wonder, Gretchen thought, that most of them die of coronaries. The way Dr. Wylie had, quite suddenly, leaving a large practice to his assistant, who had meant to do heart research but instead might someday die himself for lack of it.

But whoever would have thought, she said to herself, speeding to answer the cry "Nurse, Nurse...," whoever would have thought that I'd be drinking coffee early in the morning with Dr. Whitney, alone. She tried to think what it was he'd been whistling. The air was familiar, but she couldn't quite.... Oh, yes, *The Girl I Left Behind Me.*"

"Nurse. . . ."

Chapter 7.

IF NELLE GIBSON was a confusion to her mother, she was one to herself, too. At times it seemed as if she were two halves of a person. . . . One half was dutifully unchanging—the half that had tried for unsuccessful years to be beautiful, saw to it that neither her mother nor her studies were neglected, and in general took care that she behaved as a rather square girl who looked as though she'd be good at field hockey should behave. The other half, which she only nervously admitted to herself, was concerned with a series of rapidly shifting, glamorously unsuitable notions of what she could be if the first half were somehow disposed of.

It was this mystical second half which had led to her early investigation of astronomy—for stars had two qualities the hidden Nelle most admired. They were beautiful; they were far away. Her sober half soon admitted that astronomy concerned itself only remotely with stars and was an entirely too difficult study. But the erratic half had then summoned up a vision of Nelle, Angel of Light in the dark fastness of the mountains. During her first year in the hospital, she realized with despair that the undependable dreamer within had relinquished all responsibility for getting her there. Once again, the careful half took over. "Whatever *she* wants to do," it scoffed, "is bound to end in trouble. You take my advice and go through with this training. You might as well be a nurse as anything else. Unless you plan to be a movie star? Ha, ha. Oh, and while you're at it, you'd better continue this paean to the mountains, or you'll be getting a reputation for frivolity." And the solid half subsided, smugly aware that appearances were on its side, that frivolity would be as soon applied to a wall of cement blocks as to Nelle Gibson.

Now, in her third year, Nelle was quite independently pleased with her status as a nurse. But the long-dormant agitator was beginning to stir again. She had, in fact, quite reared to attention at the advent of Gretchen's Wally. "Gretchen's Wally, my friend," the sober side emphasized. "Bear it in mind." But the other stretched suavely, prepared to move in on the field. She'd already created a fracas on the floor. Heaven knew what other surprises lay in store. Nelle waited in rather delighted apprehension.

She was getting ready to go on duty Sunday afternoon when Gretchen knocked and came into her room.

"Nelle, I wanted to ask you something."

"All right."

"It's about this dance next Saturday. Have you made any plans about that?"

"No. No, I haven't."

"I thought perhaps you'd like Wally to take you."

"Why, Gretchen," Nelle laughed nervously. "This is so seldom...."

"Don't be silly. You like him, don't you?"

74

"Oh, for goodness sakes. . . . Yes, I like him. But I don't want him asked to ask me to a dance."

Gretchen blandly refused to understand. "That's not the point. He doesn't know there is one, so I just thought I'd tell him."

"Doesn't it occur to you that he'd rather take you?"

"No, he doesn't. I can't go anyway. Unless I went early."

"Neither can I. Unless I went late."

"Well, it's always better to go late. I'd be too tired to dance and then work all night, but it's all right the other way around. Wally loves to dance, you know. And he likes you. I'm sure he'll be delighted."

"Gretchen, stop it. I don't want you to ask him," Nelle said desperately.

Gretchen reflected. "How about this? I'll call and tell him about the dance, but I'll tell him I can't go. Nothing else. Then I'll bet he asks you anyway."

"You ought to be running a lonely hearts' club," Nelle complained. But it was hopeless, and she knew it. When Gretchen determined to be charitable, no entreaties reached her ears. "Do you absolutely promise not to say anything about me?"

"Of course I promise. If I say I won't, I won't. How about it?"

Nelle felt like asking what urge there was in Gretchen that prompted her to be forever giving. She gave her clothes, her men, her money, the time of her friends, her own time. It always seemed odd to Nelle, whose conception of beauty was that it took. But there was something—a grand manner—in Gretchen which made you answer all her questions and at the same time ask none. The benevolent baroness, Nelle accused her silently, nodding agreement as she reached down to tie her newly whitened shoes, brush a light film from her fingers, pin a cap on her unremarkable hair. "All right, Gretchen. Only . . . remember."

"It's nice for Wally to have someone to talk to," Gretchen went on, as though the matter were settled. "I never can get interested in all those mouldy civilizations of his. He got awfully upstage because I thought Bucephalus was a Roman general."

"Who was he?"

"A horse. Alexander the Great tamed him when he was very young. Alexander, I mean. I don't know about Bucephalus. And Alexander was Greek, so I got low marks all around."

"But I don't know things like that."

"I know you don't. But you're interested, and that's what Wally wants. At least, the other day you seemed to be, and very few people can tell the difference."

"I was. I think he's awfully interesting."

"I have a little sister, Prudence, who's crazy about horses," Gretchen went on irrelevantly. "She said last summer that if she ever owns a horse she's going to call him Bucephalus. There's a bit named after him, too, the thing that goes in the horse's mouth. But I learned that too late to impress Wally. Oh, there're all sorts of reasons why Wally and I just don't get along. All that traveling of his. I just have no wanderlust at all. My father says he and I have stayinlust. We just like to get somewhere and stay there. . . ."

Nelle shook her head wonderingly. "I can't understand that. Traveling must be . . . heaven."

Gretchen spread her hands. "You see. Made for each other, you are."

Nelle flushed, but Gretchen, who was going on about Wally, didn't notice. It was almost as if she were trying to sell him, but that didn't seem quite credible to Nelle. You don't point out the perfections of a work of art. You produce it, and it speaks for itself. She flushed again at her own line of thought.

"Wally reminds me of the dying families of English aristocracy," Gretchen observed. "I mean, he'd be so much more real playing billiards in lace cuffs than motoring in J. Press flannels, don't you think?"

"I think I have to go on the floor. Right now."

After Nelle left, Gretchen, feeling quite pleased with herself, went to her own room for a nickel and then to the phone at the end of the hall. She'd do it just as Nelle asked. But, she said to herself, I bet anything it works out my way. The way to a man's heart is through his hobbies, and Nelle was well on her way the other afternoon, only she didn't know it. It would be, she thought, the best possible solution to Wally, who, nice though he was (she always had a compulsion to qualify) was beginning to bore. In order to be boring, she realized, a person need not be dull. He just has to be interested in all the things you are not. Which would explain Wally's restlessness with her lately. Although, she thought with artless self-confidence, a man is always willing to forgive a lot for looks, which is why Wally keeps hanging around.

She dropped her nickel in the slot and dialed Operator. Waiting for Wally to answer, she hummed absently, "*I'm lonesome since I crossed the hill, and o'er the moor and valley . . .*" and wondered how Donal Banning was.

On Monday, Nelle awoke and lay for a while thinking that, after all, while these hours did away with your evenings, mornings were wonderfully improved without alarm clocks. Glancing at her own, she saw it was just past nine.

Her eyes traveled on, to the gingham-hung window, picture-plastered bureau, flung-open door of a disheveled closet, then automatically dropped as they encountered Aunt May's still life of assorted toys Nelle had owned years before. Aunt May Lofting, her mother's sister, had sporadic periods of "enriching" herself through hobbies, and the results were firmly presented

77

to her family, Aunt May's own home remaining free from the fruition of painted china, oils of sentimental scenes, minute hooked rugs of quaint derivation, and other mementoes of enrichments past. She always referred to herself as "Jason Lofting's relict," and was considering, at the moment, launching into business. "A little shop of my own," she'd say. "A knitting shop—they're always so colorful aren't they? Or a really ladylike tea-room, you know, with mature waitresses." In smocks, thought Nelle's mother. But she tried to look on the best side of her sister's ventures. "At least," she said of the tearoom, "She won't be able to give it to one of us when it goes out of business." And she gloomily contemplated a screen in her guest room on which Aunt May had painstakingly appliquéd varicolored sequins with dazzling results. "I hope she doesn't call the tearoom Chez May," said Nelle, "Oh, *don't*," cried Mrs. Gibson.

Nelle kept the canvas of dolls and balls hanging in her room, but she'd made no covenant to look at it.

"Gibson! Telephone for Gibson. . . ."

Nelle sprang hastily to the door. "All right, all right, I'll be there," she called in a loud whisper, hoping too many sleepers hadn't recognized and cursed her name. She grabbed a robe, ran down the hall belting it.

"Hello, mother," she said breathlessly.

"My dear girl," Wally protested. "Don't ever call me that unless you mean it".

"Oh. Oh, my goodness. I was just thinking about my Aunt May, so naturally I thought you were mother. . . . I mean, she's mother's sister, and nobody else ever calls me. I mean. . . ." I shouldn't have said that, she thought remorsefully. It sounds so silly. True enough, but you don't have to dash around telling the truth about everything. It was so exhilarating to have Wally call that she hardly listened to his words.

". . . and so, I suddenly thought, well now, how about asking the little Gibson Girl?" There was silence. "Well, will you?"

"Will I. . . .?" Nelle's voice wavered off, unsure. It would be awful to accept an invitation to the dance, which she suddenly recalled, if he hadn't been speaking of that at all. The wholly novel charm of being called a "Gibson Girl" seemed to have scattered her wits for sure.

"Nelle, are you attending to me at all?"

"Oh, yes, Wally," she breathed.

"I'm asking you to go to that dance next Saturday with me. The astonishing Gretchen phoned last night to tell me there's a dance, only she can't go." He laughed a little.

Nelle groaned audibly, and Wally laughed again. "Don't sigh, Nelle. I was going to ask you to go somewhere this week anyway, so this just gave me a good opportunity. How about it?"

"I'd love it, Wally."

"Good. Now, when's your day off this week?"

"It's . . . today," Nelle admitted, wishing she could have said tomorrow, or Wednesday, so as not to sound so anxious.

"Is it? Gretchen said she thought Friday."

"I'm on a different floor now. That was last week."

"Oh, well, good. It's a marvelous day. Would you like to take a run down to the museum in New York?"

This can't be happening to me, Nelle thought. I'm pampering myself with a specially lacy dream. But even in her dreams, Nelle had never fashioned for herself so elegant a young man as Wally. Being practical, she'd stayed within her limits, making her dream man only a slight improvement over the rare dates she'd known. A little handsomer, a little more stimulating than the two or three people who'd taken her out for not very interesting evenings. Once, she recalled, bowling. Once on a long subway ride to a rather bewildering party of complete strangers in the Bronx. These infrequent men had now merged into a single figure who bore no slightest resemblance to Wally.

But an hour or so later, sitting with Wally in his car, rolling along beside the broad, bright, crinkling river into the city, she said to herself it was true, if for no other reason than that she couldn't possibly have made him up.

She'd learned a little about him already. That he was twenty-four years old, that he lived with a cousin who was a lawyer, that he was perfectly independent financially, thanks to a grandfather who'd disliked both his parents. "They're divorced," Wally explained. "Dad lives in California and Mother in France. They figured that was as far away from each other as they could get without trying space ships." She divined that he was amiable toward both his parents and got along nicely without them. And that he wasn't much ruffled by Gretchen's defections. She thought, with a slight inward contraction, that Wally had schooled himself well to get along with or without anyone.

"Don't bruit this about," he was saying, "but I'm really not the idler my friends will assure you I am. I'm planning," he lowered his voice, "to write my memoirs. Naturally, I'll have to wait a good while, because nobody's interested in recollections not written at an advanced age. But I have lots of notes. I'd show them to you if I thought you could make them out, but I can't myself. I'm also going to write a book on Egyptian literature and religion. . . . A harsh people, as Gretchen rightly complains, but they have their fascinations. . . ."

He spoke with a careful avoidance of solemnity, yet Nelle felt quite sure he meant what he said, had no doubt that he'd write the book, no doubt that his seemingly aimless travel was as meaningful as a migrating bird's. She had an unusual, for her, sense of understanding more than was said.

Wally, for his part, found her warm complete attention as sweet a fire as any at which he had ever warmed his hands. He noticed with surprise that her eyelashes were very stubby and thick and her eyes a true grey, like dove's feathers.

"Have you told Gretchen about your book?" Nelle asked as they turned off the parkway and headed east.

"No. Somehow I never got around to it."

But he'd gotten around to telling her the first time, Nelle thought happily. Wally seemed to realize the same thing, because he smiled a little and then put his right hand briefly on hers. They rode in silence then for several blocks.

"My mother," Nelle observed when the car was winding through the park, "claims she's never been west of Central Park except in a car, but I don't know whether to believe her." She hugged herself at Wally's laugh.

They went to the Museum, where Wally guided her through a labyrinth of faded mummies, jewels still glowing with color, massive broken statues whose flat unsubtle lines suggested in an indefinable way the patient suffering sculptors who'd carved them in a hot valley thousands of years before. Shapely bowls and pitchers richly painted beneath their beautiful glaze stood cracked in glass cases, with a waiting about their stillness, as though silent centuries in the pyramids still lingered in them with purpose.

"You know," said Nelle, pursing her lips as she studied the vases, "I think I'll get my Aunt May to come down here with me." She nodded her head thoughtfully.

"Why?"

"Because they might keep her from opening a tearoom."

"They might what?"

Nelle gave a brief description of Aunt May astride a hobby-horse. "It was screens covered with sequins for nearly a year." She decided, at Wally's shudder, not to go into detail. "Now it's a tearoom, or maybe a knitting shop, but Mother says it will waste a lot of her capital if she actually goes ahead, because of course it's bound to fail. Aunt May would never stay interested enough to keep it going. I just thought, this pottery is so beautiful, or the jewelry. If I showed it to her, I think she'd forget the tearoom."

"It might work. After all, a potter's wheel should be fairly easy to get, where a shop might take ages," Wally offered. Nelle could see he'd grasped the essence of Aunt May very quickly.

They walked down Fifth Avenue to the Zoo then. That was Nelle's suggestion.

With Wally, Nelle felt somehow tapering, felt that her clothes were crisp and pretty, that there were lights in her hair, air beneath her feet. And somehow, when she walked with Wally, all these things were true.

The sea lions arched wetly glistening from the water of their round tank, flowed looping into the depths as the water swayed above them. They climbed, flat-flippered, with swinging necks, to the hot stone slabs where they honked earnestly and slid again without a splash into their beloved element. The sea lions played for their audience. The great cats, rippling back and forth behind bars or immobilely at rest, did not. The bears sprawled on their backs or lumbered over short crags with an appearance of clumsiness.

"Bears are very deceptive," Nelle said, watching a brown lump of shaggy fur amble pigeon-toed after a squirrel.

"How's that?"

"They have a reputation for being playful. Teddy bears and all. But look at their mean little eyes. And they seem so clumsy, but when you watch, you find they're never awkward. It's funny. . . ."

"That's the point of a reputation. If it's convincing enough, you needn't bother living up to it. You needn't bother trying to live it down either."

The children laughed and cried. They clung to their mothers, ran from their mothers, demanded, shrieked, laughed again. The sound of their voices pushed at the ears. It was the high piercing treble over the bass of the lion's roar, the bird's call, the parent's call. The children liked the monkeys and the elephants best. "Because," said Wally, "monkeys are an excellent size for children, and besides they misbehave so splendidly, and no one can do a thing about it. And elephants are so tremendous, so very much bigger than even the biggest father, but a small boy with a peanut has an elephant under his thumb, so to speak. That's very satisfying." He spoke as though this particular satisfaction had once been very real to him.

They had tea at the Plaza, and they talked and talked. Nelle, stirring her tea, glancing out the window at the carriage horses lined near the entrance to the Park, looking back to Wally's smooth round face, thought she'd never taken such pleasure in talking before. Why this, she thought, is a real conversation. I've never had one in my life till now. I've said yes please, and no thank you, and are you sure you're quite comfortable, but I've never really had a conversation. The things she said, the things she thought of, delighted her—as though they came from someone else, from that inside, always-hidden Nelle, who now seemed to be taking over altogether.

And Wally, whether he discussed the mummification of cats (so that the woman at the next table pushed her tea away with a little gasp), the few stern fairy tales found in the literature of Egypt, or the fact that his cousin, the attorney, couldn't read Jonathan Swift without consulting libel laws, seemed to her the most remarkable man she'd ever known or heard of. Of course, she'd known Wally nearly two years. But he'd been, as that dull, law-abiding Nelle had so primly insisted, "Gretchen's Wally." Today he didn't seem like anybody's. Today he was his own.

"Wally," Gretchen had once said, "is an excellent windmill to tilt with, but not one to throw a bonnet over."

Did that mean, Nelle wondered, that no one should fall in love with him?

It was late when they drove out of the city. They'd had dinner and then gone to a play that no one could get seats for a month earlier.

Now, almost back to the hospital at the end of the nicest day she could remember, she looked at the frost-white moon resting in the bent black arm of a tree and thought that in one day Wally had merged the two halves of herself into a complete person. It was nice to be whole. She felt very grateful to him. She felt, really, like someone rather beautiful.

Chapter 8.

THE sun was hot as Rosemary walked down the hill. It put a warm hand on her hair. There was, just perceptibly, the odor of tar that comes much later in the summer. From the river came the call of sea gulls, the low whistle of some boat on the sun-spangled water.

She recognized a porter from the hospital, nodded smiling at him as they waited for the trolley. He stood aside to let her board when it came.

"Your day off, too, Miss Joplin?" he asked, sitting beside her after a slight hesitation. The hesitation, Rosemary thought, was a result of hospital hierarchy. She remembered Gretchen saying sometime last year, after a date with a resident, that she'd spent the entire evening rising when the doctor came into the room.

"What do you do on your day off, Harold?" she asked the porter, who sighed and said with a half smile that he worked.

"Work? You mean at home."

"No, ma'am. Wish I did. I have a job in a department store."

"You mean you work seven days a week?"

"Seven days. Gets tiresome."

"But . . . but that's awful, Harold. You'll get sick or something."

"Can't afford to do that, ma'am. I've got a stack of kids, and my wife's not strong. Work during my vacation too," he added reflectively. "No point studying it, it's just fact."

When he got off, Rosemary waved to him through the window. It seemed pretty awful. She supposed the porters didn't make much money, but it didn't seem fair for a man to have to work all the time. Not that he'd seemed sorry for himself, but still . . .

She got off within a block of the church, then walked along the wide tree-lined street, with its massive houses set far back from the sidewalks. It was an old, once grand, part of town. Here and there an iron hitching boy still stood stiffly offering his iron ring. The trees were ponderously placid, the houses gently unfashionable, fading like large old ladies in the dress of another time.

The parsonage, behind the church, was furnished still with the collected generosity of church members now decades dead. The round Jacobean table still stood in the parlor, gracefully draped with a red-plush, ball-fringed cloth. Beaded portieres separated dining room from parlor. Wax flowers were sheltered beneath a glass dome on the marble mantel. All as it was when the first minister of the new church had stood on the threshold in 1890 and given thanks for his blessings.

Her father was in the little back study, tipped aslant in his chair, pen tapping a series of chins. He was a man who long ago had come to definite conclusions, since unaltered, on all salient subjects. Upon more abstruse ones he had no opinions whatever.

"Rosemary," he exclaimed with pleasure, laying aside his pen. "My dear child, I forgot it was today you were coming. How are you?" He came around the desk, a rotund small man uttering a stiff little greeting to his only child. Rosemary kissed his smooth cheek and said yes, father, it was always Saturday that she came.

"What's the sermon tomorrow, father?" she asked, moving toward the desk.

"Ah," he trundled to her side. "Taken from Exodus. 'Bricks Without Straw' is the lesson and my theme."

"Well, you've been making them long enough," Rosemary murmured.

A glancing query touched her father's eyes, melted swiftly at approaching footsteps.

"There you are, Rosemary," said the second Mrs. Joplin, flat-footing into the room with a feather duster in her hand.

"Here I am," the girl said coolly. Her father looked dismayed.

"You'll be staying for dinner, I hope?" Mrs. Joplin invited.

"Yes, thank you."

They might have been two women who had just met and decided not to improve on the acquaintance. Dr. Joplin continued to look apprehensive. He had the art of protective coloring, immersing himself hastily in the strongest character present. With his first wife, he had come close to being gay, to laughing at a little and loving a lot his role as a shepherd and their life in the house that in those days was never quite tidy but had seemed (how had she done it?) rather enchanted. With Rosemary, he grew a bit droll, a bit pleased with himself. But with the present Mrs. Joplin, he seemed to Rosemary just a rather fat short man who seemed always on the verge of apologizing for something.

Now, in answer to a query about tomorrow's sermon, he frowned in a self-reproachful way. "I'm sorry to say it isn't finished, I, ah. . . ." With an arch smile, he added jocularly, "I find myself guilty of slackness. To the desk!" He made as if to charge, seizing his pen.

"You could come into the kitchen with me, Rosemary, while

87

your father finishes his work." Mrs. Joplin went through the door.

Yes, and I could walk out of here and never come back, the girl thought. But she trailed Mrs. Joplin back down the narrow hall, along the worn flowery carpet, to the kitchen with its brown wood wainscoting, huge hooded gas stove, scuffed marbleized linoleum. The rich spiciness of simmering pot roast had been perceptible even in the study. Mrs. Joplin could certainly cook.

"Rosemary," she said now, lifting the lid and sniffing proudly, "Your father and I feel it would be a good time today to discuss your plans."

"Plans?"

"Surely you have plans?"

"Not that I know of."

"But . . . that's not possible. You'll be graduating in a few weeks."

"I know."

"What are you going to do then?"

Rosemary lifted her shoulders a little. "Something will turn up." She knew that an attitude of improvidence was excruciatingly maddening to her stepmother and watched, with an element of pleasure, that slight shrug do its work. Mrs. Joplin laid down the wooden spoon she'd just picked up, fixed her eyes on Rosemary.

"Rosemary," She hesitated. "This attitude is . . . not becoming."

Rosemary said nothing.

"In the workaday world, it isn't possible to wait for 'something to turn up.' Haven't you realized that yet?"

"My mother always waited."

At the mention of Rosemary's mother, Mrs. Joplin's eyes dropped. She turned away, began collecting dishes silently.

88

Then she backed through the swinging door. It slapped to and fro behind her. The sound of silver being taken from the buffet came to Rosemary's ear and the muffled padding of Mrs. Joplin's difficult feet moving around the table.

After dinner, always a noon meal for the Joplins, Dr. Joplin, more assured for the good food he'd had, reproduced the question.

"Well, dear," he said tentatively, "have you thought at all what you'll be doing after next month?"

Mrs. Joplin rested her glance on the tablecloth, firmly non-participant. In the short silence that followed, Rosemary registered the sound of water dripping hurriedly from a kitchen tap, the dallying clatter of children on the path leading to the church auditorium, a few desultory afternoon bird calls.

"Why is everybody so interested in what I'm to do?" she asked abruptly.

Mrs. Joplin, as though suddenly aware of the wasting water, the waiting children, pushed back her chair and hurried from the room.

"She's . . . your stepmother . . . is organizing a little play for the children," Dr. Joplin said. "It's really very charming. Based on a Celtic legend." As his daughter made no reply, he added with a kind of entreaty, "She does wonderfully well with children." He sighed into the silence, his rubicund face seeming to lengthen.

I don't care, Rosemary was saying to herself, I don't care. Why should he always make me feel sorry for him? I didn't marry her. Why did he have to marry *her*? The inescapable thought presented itself that she'd have disliked anyone else as much. I must be getting a sense of judgment, she thought blankly. Maybe it's from being around Preston so much. She'd never heard Preston disparage anyone. The nearest he came to it was to laugh. She remembered him smiling the day Mrs. Mew had publicly reprimanded him for laziness, though the gardens were no province of hers. "Poor woman," Preston had said, shaking his head as Mrs. Mew jerked angrily away. "Consumed in her own acid."

"Good heavens, Preston," Rosemary had asked impatiently, "Don't you ever get angry? Do you *like* everybody?"

"Not a bit of it, Miss Joplin. But anger and dislike are strong emotions. I reserve them for strong occasions. She's," he indicated with his head the door through which Mrs. Mew had erupted, "one of the weak ones. I can't be bothered."

Not, thought Rosemary now, twisting a fork, aware of her father's waiting attitude, that Mrs. Joplin is a weak one. But Preston would find something. . . .Or Dr. Grafton would.

"There aren't any concerts in New York this time of year, are there, father?" she asked.

Unprepared, her father looked blank. "Why," he said, "I'm not sure. I guess. . . .There's a very fine organist coming here next week. Perhaps you'd like to attend one of his recitals?"

"When is he playing?"

"Wednesday and Thursday night. Pieter Vandebruck. I'm sure you would . . ."

"Vandebruck? Gosh. I'm sure I would too, only I work those nights."

"Oh, what a pity. Well, I think I could arrange for you to sit in the church while he practiced some morning. He'll be staying here," Dr. Joplin added, softly proud of this.

"When did you say?"

"As he arrives here Monday evening, I presume you'd have an opportunity to hear him any morning after that till Thursday. He and I are old friends," he added unexpectedly.

"Why. . . .Well, my goodness, father. I didn't know that."

"Yes. We went to college together. Pieter came from Holland to study for the Ministry here, but he was more drawn to music than to the pulpit. We've remained friends, in absentia, as it were."

"That's perfectly wonderful. You never mentioned it."

"I thought I might have. It will be good to see him." Dr. Joplin rose. "I have about another hour's work on my sermon. You'll be here after that?"

"No. But I'll come in to say good-by when I've finished the dishes. And I'll try to get over to hear . . . your friend practice next week, if you think he wouldn't mind."

"Oh my, no. I'm sure he wouldn't. Pieter always liked an audience of any size."

"Say good-by to Mrs. Joplin for me, father."

He started to protest but after all only nodded and went into what he liked to think of as his sanctum. You couldn't, he thought, force a girl to call someone "mother." He thought, too, that the time had long passed when his wife would have welcomed it. Then, in order to escape the problems of those close to him, he plunged into a treatise on the probable problems of his parishioners. Only, he realized, picking up his pen, Rosemary never did tell us what her plans are, if any. I don't know my daughter very well. . . . Sometimes he thought that for a minister he really didn't know anyone very well.

He wrote, "Go ye, get you straw where ye can find it. . . ."

As she went by the open windows of the basement auditorium, Rosemary heard a child's voice saying with wryly solemn emphasis, "Is it awake or asleep I am, or dreaming entirely?"

She peeked cautiously in, stooping beside a vine of morning glory with folded buds. There, in the bare room she remembered so well, with its chairs stacked against the walls, its old random boards now surprisingly waxed, (what is she trying to do with her cleaning, cleaning, cleaning, Rosemary wondered. Trying to show how much better she can do things than my mother could?) were the children, assembled on the modest stage. Mrs. Joplin stood beneath, watching closely, a smile on her sallow face. Ah, thought the watcher, she smiles brightly enough for these. Why not at my father or even at me? But she brushed that aside. She wanted no smiles from this Mrs. Joplin. She was quite unaware that her father received them.

On the stage, the boy who had trebly wondered if he was dreaming entirely lay on the floor, elbow crooked, head on palm, grinning crookedly at the circle of children around him.

"Now, Aaron," said Mrs. Joplin, coming forward. "You must give a better idea of drowziness than that. Whoever heard of a man falling under a spell with such a grin on his face? And you other children, please move to the rear of the stage. There are only Michael and the Foam Maiden in this scene. Michael is to fall gradually asleep under the enchantment woven by the merrow." She turned toward a small slim girl waiting, with poise, for Michael to stop clowning and fall asleep. "I think, Margaret, we'll go on, supposing Aaron to have said his lines properly...."

Aaron, as the bewitched Michael, promptly dropped his head to the floor with a thud, squeezing his eyes tight, while the irrepressible grin widened. The watching children regarded him with delight but quickly sobered at a glance from the directress.

Margaret, white and gold as a Foam Maiden indeed, moved forward lissomely, stood swaying over the determinedly recumbent victim. She raised her supple arms and chanted in a high sweet voice,

> "By the wild white sea horses that no man can master
> By the blown spray that flies o'er the reefs of disaster,
> Let slumber enfold him. . . .
> Chain him and hold him. . . ."

She stepped closer, looking down with imperious scorn at Michael, who cautiously scratched his leg and then lay still.

"You who are holding a merrow in thrall,
Did you not know I would hear the waves call?"

Rosemary backed away from the window, wiping a bit of dirt from the hem of her yellow dress. It was apparent to the most biased eye that Mrs. Joplin was enjoying herself and that the children were too. Well, so what, she thought defiantly. She cooks and cleans and loves children, and probably dogs love her. But so what? I don't love her.

The return trolley swung clattering along. After a while she could see the hospital, spread low on the hilltop, with a fringe of trees bordering it, and above, the pure brow of the sky, cloudless, serene.

Chapter 9.

"MY dearest sister Gretchen," Prudence wrote. "I wait every day for a letter from you, but as nothing ever comes except suggestions from Winkleman's that I take advantage of their eight-day sale (and does Winkleman's, I wonder, have any idea of my financial situation?), I've decided that, in order to spur our correspondence, I'll have to take my Underwood in hand and initiate one." Gretchen smiled, then frowned, because this time Prudence had written on the reverse side of some mimeographed sheets, and her letter was harder than usual to read. Prudence saved all her pocket money and baby-sitting money for her horseback riding. Writing paper she considered an extravagance if there was anything around short of stones that she could print on. "Let me know frankly," she wrote, "if you find this letter difficult, and next time I'll use old newspaper. Nothing special marches itself at home, and this is mainly to say *please* come here this summer. Mother said you were thinking of only a week or two and then going back to work. If not for the sake of all of us, who want you, consider your health. You may look strong as an ox, but even an ox has to rest sometime. Speaking of cattle, you should have seen the sad hack they made

94

me ride the other day. I got to the stable so late that everything was out but this tired old fatty with a torso like a hogshead who turned out to be a single footer. Well, you know my opinions on that. I'd as soon ride an armchair. The stable man said they give you a comfortable ride, but I said they give you an undignified seat. I won't tell you what he said to that. *Please* come, for the whole summer. Dad actually took us out to the lodge (we must *not* go on calling it a cabin) last weekend. The drive was beautiful, and the lake looked simply dreamy, though I must say the lodge itself sort of ran to damp and cobwebs. We opened all the windows and doors to air it out, and Dad went wandering about hungrily, looking for a place to lie down I guess. But of course the hammock wasn't there, and Dad's too lazy to go as far down as the ground. You can imagine how anxious he's getting even to drive us out there at all. He said a hundred times (yes, at *least*) how he hoped you'd be with us this summer. I suppose partly because you wait on him even better than mother does. William has a girl. She's a freshman at Northwestern and her first name is Sheridan. I won't comment further because I hope by the time you get here she'll be nothing but a sad memory. After all, William must have *some* sense of humor left. Hally's changed so you'll hardly know her. She locks the bathroom door and puts on mudpacks and giggles when boys are around. She's still getting A's in everything, I must admit. Have to go now. Noah is invited to a birthday party, and Mom says I should supervise while he cleans up. You know Noah, he washes his face as if it were made of tissue paper. It's a girl's birthday, but he bought her a model airplane and plans to show her how to put it together. I can't say too much against him either, because he saddle-waxes my boots for a nickel. Have to go really. Mother says give you her love. Dad just hollered up when are you coming home. When are you? Love and xxx, Pru."

Gretchen grabbed a piece of paper, scribbled hurriedly, "I'll go back with Mom after graduation and spend the summer. I wanted to anyway but needed a little coaxing. Ask Dad why he doesn't come East and see his eldest born dubbed. I'll send a scout to break trail, if he wants, or hire litter bearers."

She mailed the letter in the hospital entrance hall. Then, having nothing else to do, went into the Coffee Shop for a frosted.

Dr. Bradley was sitting at the counter drinking a chocolate malted and eating cookies. She smiled at Gretchen, who swung onto the next stool, shaking her head disapprovingly at what seemed to be the doctor's lunch.

"I'll have a frosted, Bitsy," she said to the counter girl, and then, "I guess there aren't any other people who take such poor care of themselves." This to the doctor.

"As doctors, you mean?"

"Mmm. Do you eat this sort of lunch every day?"

"Only when I'm lucky."

"That's terrible." As she spoke, Gretchen thought that Dr. Bradley was one of the few physicians in the hospital who could talk freely to anybody without seeming to fear she'd compromise her dignity.

"I'm too busy," the doctor was saying, "to stop in the middle of the day for food. I thought when I was an intern that the work was hard, but it's nothing compared to private practice."

"I suppose once you start to be a doctor, you just can't stop. There was a doctor at home who wanted to give up her practice, and she had to move out of town for a year before she could manage it." They drank for a little while, and then Gretchen went on, "We all liked your last lecture very much."

"That's good. I really do think nurses are in a position to do enormous good with children."

"Won't work, of course," Gretchen said absently, immediately regretting the words. But Dr. Bradley took her up very seriously, so with a sigh of exasperation at herself, she explained. "Well, it's this way, Dr. Bradley. It's fine to want us, the nurses, I mean, to put everything that appears relevant on the charts. I have no doubt in the world that it would be very useful too. But there are so darn many things against it that I'm afraid it'll all have to remain just a good idea." The doctor showed no sign of letting her off. "Look, in the first place, we're so rushed that we feel glad to get T.P.R's and anything really glaring charted. And to go on with . . . well, of course this isn't true of all the doctors, but. . . ." She stopped.

"Go on, go on, I'm not going to rush off in a dudgeon."

Since there was no help for it, Gretchen went on, assuring herself that the next time she opened her mouth she'd hold her foot down hard. "It's been our experience that if you put anything beyond what the doctors feel is absolutely necessary on the charts, most of them throw a fit." In spite of herself she spoke defiantly, with the recollection clear in her mind of peevish doctors tossing down charts on which some nurse (usually a student, the graduates were too experienced) had conscientiously recorded things that seemed to her important but which apparently seemed to the doctors just that much more to read. "My God," one of them had said, "What is this girl, a nurse or a novelist? She's got everything on here but the color of the patient's toothbrush. . . ."

Dr. Bradley finished her lunch but remained a moment, staring into the chocolate-coated depths of her glass. "Well," she said at length, "perhaps that's so. Of course, everybody's too rushed. Nurses, doctors, everybody. But I still think the nurses should report as much as possible. What would you think . . . how about a planned guide for chart recording? Something the nurses could study and use as a reference when needed? It could be presented to the Medical Staff for an O.K. by the Chiefs of Surgery and Medicine. Something like that?" She reached for her bag and stood up. "Does it seem at all reasonable?"

97

"It seems perfectly reasonable," Gretchen said earnestly. Only it won't work, she added to herself. Bradley is different from the rest. Everything, even a record, is alive to her . . . everything's capable of change, improvement, readjustment. But even the word "readjustment" would send most of the Staff and the entire Board into a decline. No, she thought, it would be a long time before a constructive change would have a chance of survival in the hospital.

Dr. Bradley looked at her watch. "Oh, good heavens, goodby," she gasped and raced away.

As she was in the Coffee Shop and out of uniform, Gretchen lit a cigarette. Then she went on with her thoughts about charts. The whole thing, really, had its ludicrous side. The fact that the nurse must never state a conclusion. She must always say, "It appears" or "It would seem." The patient could be crying hard enough to launch himself, but the nurse wrote "Patient appears to be crying" or, more formally, "There seems to be a diffusion from the lachrymal glands." That, of course, was a legality. Nurses can't diagnose. But there'd been some awfully funny things written on the charts, again usually by the students. There was the time, now legend, when Rosemary, who wouldn't use the word "belch" and didn't know the word "eructation" had written in her careful hand, "The patient seems to be passing air by mouth." The intern had roared with laughter and spread the story throughout the building.

She didn't realize Rosemary was in the Coffee Shop until she turned and found her sitting in Dr. Bradley's vacated place.

"Coke, I guess," Rosemary said to Bitsy. "Hi, Gretchen."

"What's the matter? You look funny."

"Mr. Consella."

"Who's Mr. Consella?" Really, Gretchen thought, I never knew anyone who had to be helped along with a conversation the way Rosemary does. It was irritating sometimes, but at

98

other times, as now, Gretchen was caught by the current of sadness that was part of Rosemary's voice even when she was laughing. She seemed to have none of the casual but occasionally tugging strings that tie people to something solid, so they can kite about freely, aware of a base. She never made offhand references as Nelle and Gretchen did to what her father thought of the President, what she'd done as a little girl in the summer, whether her grandmother was the kind who made gingersnaps or the kind who organized drives. Gretchen, baffled as well as touched, now found her generally ready source of advice and encouragement dry. "Who's Mr. Consella?" in a warm voice was the best she could do.

"He's. . . . He was . . . on Men's Surgical. Last night," Rosemary hesitated, biting her lip, as she always did when nervous, "last night, when I went in to him, about eight o'clock, there he was, sitting up in bed like a bright little bird. He was an old man, Gretchen. Such a . . . such a *clean* old man. He was awfully nice. He said they hadn't made him his eggnog, so I told him I'd whip one up in the diet kitchen, and when I got back with it, he was dead. Just like that. . . ."

Gretchen felt at an utter impasse. After three years of training, it just didn't seem possible that Rosemary should take a death, even the death of a nice old man, so bitterly. You just couldn't do it. Repeated reactions of this sort result only in disaster to the service of other patients as well as to the personality of the nurse. That's what Miss Merkle had said in a Nursing Arts class, and it was true.

"It was a good way to die, for an old man," Gretchen said, uttering the old, old words of comfort without much hope. Because she thought it was the death, more than it's being Mr. Consella's, that grieved Rosemary. She can't stand it, Gretchen thought. And then, no, what she can't stand is sudden death. That's why she was so unhappy in the Accident Room. She's all right if she expects it. But if she's going to be able to go on with nursing, she'll have to take it both ways. Suddenly unable to tolerate longer the brooding atmosphere, she slipped off the stool.

"I really have to run, Rosemary. Unless," she lingered restlessly, "Unless you think I could help?" But Rosemary shook her head, and Gretchen fled ashamed of her relief.

Rosemary remained, realizing with a small sense of shock that relief of Gretchen's. I don't blame her, she said to herself, as if this would make Gretchen's flight more acceptable. It didn't. She didn't, in truth, blame Gretchen in the least, but saying so did nothing to lessen the hurt. She put a nickel on the counter and twisted it with her finger, five circles one way, five circles the other.

Bitsy, the girl behind the counter, watched her curiously. Bitsy knew everyone in the hospital, and had opinions on all of them. It would have come as a surprise to the medical staff, most of whom didn't recognize her when they met on the street. "Unless," as she told the counter man, "I carried a coke and a cheese on rye when I went downtown. Then one of the high and mighties might know who I was." The counter man shrugged. He knew the vaguely disturbed nods of nurses and doctors he greeted on the street when he wore his pin stripe and snapbrim in place of the Coffee Shop whites. He got a kick out of knowing they'd go along puzzling about him for a couple of blocks and then fail to make a connection next day when he served them the blue-plate special. "The nurses probably think we're old patients, and the doctors think we're patients who aren't coming to them any more." He sounded pleased.

Bitsy, watching Rosemary toy with the nickel, was glad she hadn't decided to be a nurse. Not that she could have anyway, because Bitsy had left school the day she was legally permitted to. Still, if she *had* finished school, she might have gone into training, so it was probably just as well she hadn't. This comfortable reasoning allowed her to study Rosemary with a certain kindly sympathy. Poor thing, she said to herself, wondering when the nickel would be released for the cash register. Goes around looking like a chewed string, hasn't got a fella, and even Miss Bemis got tired of sitting with her. And Miss Bemis was one of the nicest students in the whole place. Miss Bemis, in fact, was the reason Bitsy sometimes thought she might have been a nurse. Beautiful, she was, always gay looking, dates all the time. . . . Bitsy sighed, looked quickly back at Rosemary. Poor, poor thing, she thought.

Dr. Grafton was coming in. Bitsy drew a cup of black coffee without being asked. These interns, she mused lovingly. Sometimes they sold their blood for money, she'd heard. Bitsy would have bet they'd produce more caffeine than corpuscles.

"Thanks, Bitsy," Dr. Grafton said, giving her his crinkly-eyed smile as he sat beside Rosemary.

Well, thought Bitsy, Joplin sure lit up for him. You wouldn't know it was the same girl. Of course, Dr. Grafton seemed to go out of his way for people who looked sad or nervous. She'd heard a lot about how much time he spent talking to unhappy patients, like Mrs. Parker on O.B. that lost her baby. Bitsy had seen Mrs. Parker leaving that morning with her husband. She hadn't looked exactly wild with joy, but she'd been smiling at her husband in a slow way, and Dr. Grafton had seen them both to the hospital door, shaking hands with the husband, who'd practically torn the doctor's off, and waving good-by to Mrs. Parker, who'd looked so—so grateful. A couple of other interns had been talking about Dr. Grafton one day, and one of them asked if Grafton was going to specialize. Yeah, in lame ducks, the second had said, and they both laughed. But Bitsy thought he was pretty wonderful. She was glad to be able to tell herself that he was interested in Miss Joplin only because she looked like something that had been rained on for six weeks and then left in a basement.

". . . Pieter Vandebruck," Rosemary was saying. "My father says he'll be practicing mornings this week, from Tuesday to Thursday, and I just wondered. . . ."

"I don't suppose he'd want two people listening, do you?" Dr. Grafton asked.

"I think he wouldn't mind." She couldn't help smiling.

"That'd be marvelous. This is really awfully kind of you. What morning? I could make it easily on Wednesday."

"Me too. I . . . it would be a good idea if we started around nine."

"Oh, fine. Then afterwards we could have lunch. All right?"

Rosemary thought with dismay that of course Mrs. Joplin would ask them for lunch. It was the kind of thing she did. Then she'd turn out a meal that anyone else would take two days to prepare. My mother, she thought, was never able to cook, though to be sure she'd always asked people to stay for impromptu meals that were amazingly botched and usually ended in Dr. Joplin's tearing off to the delicatessen. "Oh, no," her mother would say to the guests, "It isn't too much trouble. Nothing is too much trouble." "Nothing is always too much trouble for my wife," Dr. Joplin would say drily. But he'd laugh, and her mother would laugh, and the guests would have a wonderful time eating potato salad and liverwurst. Surely, she told herself uncertainly, surely anyone would rather eat potato salad and liverwurst with my mother than sit down to a proper meal at a proper table with Mrs. Joplin?

"Isn't that all right?" Dr. Grafton was saying again.

Rosemary turned to him. "Oh yes. Only, I think my . . . my stepmother will probably invite us, if you wouldn't mind."

"Mind? I'd love it That's all settled then. Meet you in the garden at a quarter to nine. Sounds like a song, doesn't it?" He shoved back his sleeve, stared accusingly at his watch. "Two-thirty! Where'd the rest of the day go?" He disappeared before Rosemary could reply. Two-thirty? She realized with a start that she'd have to tear to be on the floor on time.

Picking up the nickel, still warm from Rosemary's fingers, Bitsy stared after her. "Well," she said to the counterman. "For a girl without any fellas, she sure handled that neat."

"Huh? Who did what? "

"Nothing. Sometimes I wish I'd finished school. . . . I could have been a good nurse, I bet."

"Got another case on a medico?"

"Oh, you go jump in a lake, " Bitsy said without much spirit.

Chapter 10.

ORIN WHITNEY shoved his worn doctor's bag (it had been Gardner Wylie's) onto the rear seat of his sedan, climbed into the driver's seat, lit a cigarette before starting the motor. As he reached for the hand brake, a splendid figure approached the parking area. Gretchen Bemis, in a biscuit-colored cotton dress, mahogany braids like a queen's hat, walked rather aimlessly toward the hospital.

Marvelous carriage, thought Dr. Whitney, letting the brake out. Then, for no apparent reason, he pressed on the foot brake, waiting.

"Give you a lift?" he called as Gretchen neared him.

Gretchen hesitated, thinking quickly. She had a couple of dollars in a change purse, but no bag, hat, or gloves. She could say she'd been going downtown and then just ride back on the trolley when he left her. A chance to ride with Dr. Whitney was not to be ignored. On the other hand, Dr. Whitney was anything but unperceptive. I'd better, she decided, just thank him, just say I'd have loved a lift only I'm not going anywhere.

"I'd love one," she said and got in beside him.

For a second before setting the car in motion, he studied the little purse in her hands, lifted his amused eyes to hers. In the space of that second a change, like the delicate alteration of a pulse beat, took their glances, so lightly met, and locked them fast. With a sort of surprise, a sort of meeting, their eyes held. So . . . ? The soft, unspoken question was an awareness between them. Is it you? Neither spoke a word.

Then with a sudden deep breath, as though to deny a question had been asked or could be answered, Dr. Whitney sent the car rolling toward town.

"Any special place I can drop you?" he asked, his generally courteous voice abrupt.

"Well, just downtown somewhere. . . ."

"I see."

He drove silently. Gretchen liked the look of his hands on the wheel, brown and long with square nails. She liked his big polished Cordovan shoes pressing the clutch, moving from accelerator to brake, and the line of his thigh under the tan gabardine suit. She hardly dared look at his face but knew what it would be. Stern now, perhaps a little stunned. Dr. Whitney, she thought, didn't like that shared glance. But he had shared it. . . .

"Look here," he said, braking for a light, "you really haven't anywhere to go, have you?" He turned to look at her, looked quickly away again, flexing his hands on the wheel.

Suddenly Gretchen felt dizzy with the sweetness of power. It was something in the air that she could breathe, could fold in her hands. This was Dr. Whitney, the big, magnificent man who nodded remotely in the halls, unconscious of the flurries he left in passing. This beside her was Dr. Whitney, afraid to look at her, for fear he'd look too long.

"No," she answered. "I just thought it would be nice . . . to have a ride. I'll go back on the trolley."

He shifted and drove on through the business section past a housing development. "You'd think they were born, not made," he remarked, looking at the endless rows of similar houses. Very noncommittal now. Then they were in the older, residential area. Gretchen saw the old grey-stone church where Rosemary's father was minister. She twisted around to see the parish house, huddled in back. Rosemary's dungeon, she thought. To which she unaccountably returns every time she has a day off. I wonder why that is?

"Did you see Donal Banning this morning?" she asked, really caring, but with part of her mind singingly unable to care for anything but the sound of his voice answering, the recollection of his brown eyes asking something else.

Dr. Whitney nodded. "He'll have to go to a cardiac convalescent home, I think. It's something I hope to arrange today. Parents don't have a dime, but we'll get the money through the sponsorship of the Heart Association."

"Will he . . . will he be all right?"

"All right? I don't know. Yes, after a long time, I suppose he'll be comparatively all right. But it's all wrong, it's just all wrong." A pause. Then, "He's a great little kid. You ask him how he's feeling, and he says 'fine.' No matter what, he says 'fine.' Dr. Bradley says he's smart as a whip. I wouldn't know. The poor little devil's been too sick to show much of anything since I was called in."

"He's Dr. Bradley's patient?"

"Yes. The parents tried liniments, aspirin, and lord knows how many bottles of growing-pain wampum, till the kid had an acute attack. Then they called Bradley in, and she called me." He shook his head. "I don't know what you can call it. Stupidity? Maybe it's fright, and it's certainly ignorance. It's. . . . There're so many things we don't know. We know what, but not why. Rheumatic fever thrives in wretched places, tenements. . . . It thrives on poor food, poor sanitation. Only why? Polio doesn't. One does, one doesn't. Well, who's to find out?

It's more important to find out why Donal Banning is ill than to cure him." He might have sounded callous, but he didn't. Angry, frustrated, he sounded both of these. "Something has to be done," he said in a flat, uninflected voice. Then with excitement rising again. "The big contribution is going to come from research." He sounded very sure of himself. Not a man to qualify, Dr. Whitney. "I laughed a little at those houses back there, looking all alike. But they're a step in the right direction. They're new, clean for the present at any rate, and they sit smack in the middle of air and sunlight. A step, but not the most important one. To know *why*. . . ." He broke off with a smiling shrug, suddenly aware of his repetitiveness.

"Well, then," Gretchen said reflectively, "Public Health would be. . . ."

"Public Health *is* research," he broke in. "Not the branch I would have chosen, but they'll have answers." He drove a while in silence. "I had thought myself, once, of filling a vacancy they had in the department of cardiology out in the big center on Long Island. Every facility, thousands of cases. I was just about to take it, but then Gardner. . . ." His words came more and more slowly, finally ceased altogether.

But here we are, thought Gretchen, unable not to be feminine, not to skip from the general to the particular, here we are. Only where are we going? He hasn't said anything more about leaving me downtown. She almost dared to think where he must be taking her, but not quite. Because what if he suddenly put on the brakes and said, "Oh, I forgot, you wanted to get off downtown. . . ." No, she decided, snugly almost secure, but prepared to be wrong, I just won't think about it at all.

They drove, not speaking now. The beelike humming of the tires was loud in the quiet of the afternoon. Then the car slowed as the doctor swung onto the gravel of a curved driveway before a huge old clapboard house. On the vast lawn, near a well, lay a white collie, who leaped to his feet, thrust slim ears forward, then galloped headlong at them.

Dr. Whitney pushed the dog back as Gretchen got out.

"Hold on, Kim," he told the cavorting, pink-tongued collie, who seemed to be under the impression that Gretchen was a long-lost friend and was frantically trying to attain her lap to show how much he'd missed her. "Say, do you two know each other?"

Gretchen shook her head, laughing. "Not unless Dollar introduced us. But I hardly think I'd forget . . . Kim, is it?"

"Kim it is. Who's Dollar? Oh yes, that animal of Miss Merkle's. I always feel like setting him loose."

"I don't think he'd go. He's . . . a friend."

"You can't be sure, even with friends. Look at Kim here, hasn't even said hello to me."

"He's too young to be constant, I guess." And at that moment, Kim, in a flailing of white legs and tail, shot around the house in pursuit of a squirrel.

Dr. Whitney waved a hand at the house. "This is my home, Miss Bemis. And office. I thought, since you had nothing to do, you might have tea with me and my father. I have to get back to the hospital in an hour or so." He looked at her for an answer. Something, perhaps the talk of medicine and the greeting of Kim, had steadied his feelings. His look was of inquiry only.

Well anyway, she thought, walking beside him, he's been . . . friendlier . . . to me than to anyone else I've ever heard of. Many an organdy graduate cap had been set for Dr. Whitney, without result, and many a student's head turned, without intention. And here am I, Gretchen said to herself with a bubbling elation, coming to tea with the doctor and his father.

The house was vast, many-roomed. Built around the close of the old century, with two large identical rooms on either side of the hall, all leading back to the service area. For family living,

Gretchen always thought this a hopelessly bad arrangement. You just naturally tended to live on one side, and it would become more or less a matter of not letting space go to waste that would lead you to the other side, and there you would sit uncomfortably till conscience allowed you to escape. For a doctor, though, it was fine. Dr. Gardner Wylie, who had left this house, his practice, and his modest fortune to Orin Whitney, had turned the left-hand rooms into an office. A large waiting room with separate entrance, a consultation room immediately off it, and treatment room (once the butler's pantry) behind that.

"I'll introduce you to Dad," Dr. Whitney said, "and then, if you'll excuse me, I have some electrocardiogram reports to look at in the office. We'll have tea in a bit, all right?"

As Gretchen nodded, the door opened, a big man entered frowning. He smiled though when he saw Gretchen and the doctor. I'd know him for Dr. Whitney's father anywhere, Gretchen thought. Grey mustache, thinning white hair, deep furrows on his brow and beside his nose, but the same brilliant brown eyes, now fixed intently on Gretchen.

"Well, how do you do?" he said approvingly, removing his hat, dropping his car keys on a table.

"This is my father. Miss Bemis, Dad. A nurse from the hospital."

"I'm glad to find you here, Miss Bemis. Are you going to work for us?"

"Oh, no," Gretchen said quickly, "I'm still a student, a senior, that is. . . ."

"I've asked Miss Bemis for tea, Dad. And don't let Kennedy hear you for lord's sake." He went on in a lower tone to Gretchen. "Kennedy is my office nurse. She and Dad disagree."

"I don't disagree with her," Mr. Whitney said. "Simply think she's in the wrong profession. She ought to be on the radio or the stage or something. Woman talks all the time. . . ."

"She's a good office nurse," his son interrupted. "What were you scowling about just now?" He turned to Gretchen. "Let's go into the living room, Miss Bemis. Have some tea with us, Dad?"

Mr. Whitney settled himself in a leather chair after seeing that Gretchen got the nicest one. "I was scowling," he said, "over the situation on the parkway. Every time your wheels turn three times you have to pay another dime. For less than this," he said sternly, "they dumped the tea in the harbor."

Dr. Whitney seemed unimpressed. "I'll see if Mrs. Morley will give us some tea. Unless it's all still in the harbor, that is."

When his son had gone, Mr. Whitney smiled at Gretchen. "Orin thinks I fuss. So I do. Sometimes I'd rather not."

"I know. You get into roles. Sometimes I think my father isn't so lazy as he pretends to be. Although I don't know," she added thoughtfully.

"Lazy, is he? Well, it's a good way to conserve. Where do you come from, Miss Bemis?"

"Cincinnati."

"Miss it?"

Gretchen nodded. "Lately I miss it an awful lot. It was marvelous to get away. But I'll be glad to go back."

"Will you practice nursing there?"

Because his questions seemed interested, not just polite, Gretchen gave herself time to consider the answer. "Well, I can't decide. I can't seem to decide what to do at all. You'd think I'd know by now, only. . . ." She broke off with a turn of the hands.

After a moment, Mr. Whitney spoke, and now there was no trace of querulousness he'd had speaking to his son. "Miss Bemis, try to remember one thing, before you make the same mistake Orin did. . . ." He shook his head regretfully. "Orin just leaped into a practice, without thinking where it would lead. Now he can't bring himself to go back and start where he should have started right after internship, if Gardner hadn't wanted him so. Oh, Gardner was a fine man, and he certainly thought the world of Orin. He had all his interests at heart, except Orin's real interest. Gardner just couldn't believe Orin would actually leave him to do research, and Orin liked Gardner too much to hurt him. He was a real doctor, Gardner was, in the sense of Hippocrates. In medicine to heal and help, not to pile up a fortune. But everyone had to help Gardner's way. He'd admit the importance of research, but he squirmed every time Orin mentioned it. Bull-headed. Brilliant, generous, but. . . ." He sighed heavily. "I suppose in a way that's why I get— crotchety—around Orin. For him to make his own contribution, he'd have to make up his mind to leave his practice and devote all his time for a year or so to cardiac study at some good teaching center. That's what he can't decide to do. It'll take something pretty—oh, I don't know—it'll take a real jolt to get him started. It's too bad. But habit seems to be stronger than even our own wishes, doesn't it?" He rubbed a light finger over his mustache, his eyes on the girl. "Well, I didn't mean to go off like this. What I wanted to say, Miss Bemis, is think carefully. The important thing in life is to have a real connection between what you're doing and what you are."

Dr. Whitney returned, carrying a tray with cups, teapot, and large ham sandwiches. He lifted his brows as he set the tray before Gretchen. "Will you pour? I apologize for the sandwiches. There didn't seem to be anyone in the kitchen, so I made them myself, only I can't bring myself to cut the crusts off bread."

"It's all right with me," Gretchen assured him. "I'm starved."

As they ate, she looked around the room. A man's room of old leather, worn orientals, two walls of books, a well-used fireplace. But a woman's touch was obvious in touches like the bowl of flowers on the mantel. What woman? Gretchen wondered. Uneasily she realized that, just because Dr. Whitney avoided nurses, it didn't follow he avoided women. Oh gosh, she mourned, suddenly uninterested in the sandwich, why did I have to think of that? Why, in fact, was she thinking this way at all? No wonder Dr. Whitney was elusive, if his merely taking a girl to tea, and that rather by accident, immediately gave rise to jealous brooding. She came out of abstraction to hear Mr. Whitney wishing he lived in the country.

"With chickens," he explained.

"I don't like chickens," his son said. "They're stupid."

"They can't help it. They've got little heads."

"I can help being around them. Except to eat, of course."

"Orin, this habit you have of demanding intelligence in everything around you is hardly the proper attitude for a doctor. Especially," he drove the barb in, "especially a doctor with a large general practice."

"But Dr. Whitney's a heart specialist," Gretchen blurted. The doctor shook his head slightly. "In a way. Mostly. But you just can't help it, other things creep in—side issues, old patients with new complaints. In a town this size, a heart man can't really specialize. The throat fellows can, and the surgeons. But Dad's right. I'm a G.P. with a large cardiac practice." He got up. "I have about half an hour's work in the office. Will that get you back in time?"

"Oh, don't hurry, Dr. Whitney. I'm not on till eleven."

He turned at the door. "Of course. I should have remembered." For a second he seemed to be remembering. His eyes on hers were intent, with the questioning surprise they'd held in the car. Then he was gone.

Mr. Whitney looked from the empty door to Gretchen, then cocked his head. Gretchen gazed steadily back at him. On their lips the touch of a smile quivered and grew.

But all Mr. Whitney said was, "I'd still like to keep chickens."

"Well, can't you?" she asked.

"I suppose I could. But so long as Orin's here, I'd like to be with him. I read books on chicken farming—the really big stuff, you know. It's pleasing me no end. Doubtless getting me to none."

"My father gets ideas like that. One year we were going to have maple syrup. Dad told everyone he knew not to buy any, and he went to our cabin over in Indiana and tapped about forty trees. It has to be done at a special time, you see, when the nights are cold and the days warm. Dad worked terribly hard. That's what made it worse, because Dad just isn't used to working hard. He says it unsettles him."

"What does he do?"

"He has a bookstore. It's one of the nicest bookstores in town, and he has it paying well enough so he can mostly sit around and gossip or read."

"Seems like a very sound man. What happened about the maple syrup?"

"Well, nothing. He'd been tapping oak trees."

Mr. Whitney shouted with laughter, and Gretchen could hardly hear herself adding, "It wouldn't have mattered anyway, because there aren't any sugar maples on our property."

"Oh, my word," sputtered Mr. Whitney, his shoulders shaking. "That's marvelous. I should think anyone would know an oak tree."

"Dad wouldn't. He's too busy with the leaves of books to notice the real thing. He says he reads poetry to educate himself, and then for relaxation he reads poetry."

"I never have figured out exactly how to go about reading poetry. It's a shame, really. But somehow I don't seem able to pick up poetry and settle down to read it, like a book, I mean. There never seems to be a proper time for poetry."

"Dad reads it any time."

"But don't you feel there should be . . . a setting or something? It seems like a different kind of reading."

113

"I don't know. I don't read it much myself any more, but when I do, I go at it the same way I would a novel. Just open the cover and start reading."

Mr. Whitney shook his head. "That's the way it should be." He sounded rather baffled. "It's the same with paintings. I went into an art gallery once, just to see what I'd do. . . ."

"What did you?"

"Well, I looked at the pictures, all right. Some were fine, and others I didn't like much. But I got through the whole place in twenty minutes. Some people who came in when I did were still on the first picture when I left. Probably I'm just not art-minded." He seemed to dislike his own diagnosis.

"I think that there are people who are art-minded but not art-educated, and then it's just a matter of opening the poetry or going back to the gallery until you're accustomed to the territory." She spoke as though this were a considered opinion, though in fact she'd just thought of it at the moment. But it felt like a sound argument, and Mr. Whitney looked suitably impressed.

"Tell me," he said, "are there any more at home like you?"

Gretchen smiled. "Plenty. I have two sisters, Prudence and Hally. Hally thinks life is pretty real and earnest. Pru feels that if you don't bring your horse back lathered, your judgment in other matters will be good."

"Younger than you?"

"Oh, yes. They all are. My brother Noah is eight, and I guess his whole life is spent explaining why he forgot again when he said *this* time he'd be sure to remember. William's nineteen. He's wonderful. . . ."

"They sound wonderful, the whole bunch," Mr. Whitney said wistfully. "Miss Bemis, I hope you'll come again and often."

"I'll do my best, sir," she answered softly, and again the unremarked-upon smile passed between them. "The flowers are pretty," she said then, indicating the bowl on the mantel.

He looked up with surprise. "Oh, yes, the flowers. Mrs. Morley, our housekeeper, puts them there all the time. It does give a nice appearance."

"It really does," Gretchen said with satisfaction.

As they drove back to the hospital, Gretchen said, "I like your father very much, Dr. Whitney."

"He's pretty fine," the doctor said. "Seemed to get along, you two."

"Oh, we had a good time, talking about nature and . . . things."

Dr. Whitney either didn't notice or ignored her hesitation. "Dad's always trying to get close to Nature. Only Nature keeps moving over," he laughed. After a while, "Don't pay any attention to the way he needles me. He's trying to get me to do what I want to do myself." He stopped for a light, stretched his arms against the wheel. There was nothing now in his manner to show that twice today he'd looked at her as if in search of something and had once looked away as though he feared to find it. But there was something else, and if it wasn't as dizzyingly sweet, it still was warm and would this morning have seemed incredible. He spoke to her of the thing which meant most to him, confident of her understanding.

Now he sat up a bit. "Don't know how I happened to forget it, but I promised Preston we'd have a couple of sets this afternoon. Whew, he'll be hopping. Our tea seemed to run away with the afternoon."

Gretchen, dreaming with contentment, said, "He's nice, Preston. Gardeners seem to make good sort of men, or is it the other way around?"

"Both, maybe. I sometimes think it's because they take out their destructive impulses on weeds. Preston's as fine as they come. He really has one of the best minds I know. And one of the best serves."

Twilight, pink and gray, like smoke, was sifting down over the lace-leaved trees, the homeward-hurrying pedestrians. Gretchen thought how it always seems as if twilight drops from the sky and morning lifts from the earth. Lying down, rising up. . . .

When they drove into the doctors' parking area, Dr. Whitney was already in his hospital mien—abstracted, casual. "It was nice," he said. "See you again."

Will you, Dr. Whitney? Gretchen asked. I hope you will. But the words were thoughts only. He said nothing about some other time they'd meet. Only, "By the way, I arranged this afternoon for the Banning child to leave. He'll probably go out tonight." With a wave of his hand, he took his bag and strode toward the hospital.

And so, thought Gretchen, I won't even get to see him on the floor. He had no other patients on Pediatrics. She felt a confusion of crazy pleasure and anxious uncertainty. It was not an unfamiliar feeling, this one, for Gretchen had been more or less falling in love since she'd been fourteen. But not like this, she thought. Nothing like this at all.

Chapter 11.

CEASELESSLY occupied with the crises of life, with the dramatic, sometimes tragic, sometimes joyous pinnacles of many lives, the hospital managed to reduce all such material to routine. Like a well-conducted business office, it introduced new matter, disposed of the old, reclaimed the damaged. The hospital itself took very good physical care of its human property, very little notice of accompanying human emotions.

But the hospital functioned every waking, every sleeping moment.

At four-thirty-five A.M., an intern puts out a fumbling hand, attains his phone, nods at the message, then, at a repeated question, croaks, "Sure, sure. Be there in a minute. Emergency." He drops the phone back, swings out of bed into his starched whites in a single motion, and strides down the hall, thoroughly awake. Not running. No one ever runs through a hospital corridor; it would look too much like terror. What the intern finds is a frightened Italian father, his six-year-old son doubled on the Emergency Room table. The little boy's face is chartreuse, beaded with perspiration. He can't talk at all, but he screams well.

At five-fifteen, the little boy, whose name is Alonzo, is sitting weakly at the edge of the table. His father, in the corridor outside where he has been banished, hears the intern's voice lifted a bit for the first time. The voice is pleading, stern, despairing. "Look, Alonzo," the doctor says, "don't you want to grow up to be a big fellow? Somebody like Larry Jansen, huh?" A small reply follows unheard by the father. The intern's voice has the tone of someone running a harried hand through his hair, "Well, Alonzo, you've got to understand. You can't go on eating nothing but coffee and this . . . this biscotta . . . or whatever you call it. Vegetables, Alonzo, meat and fruit. Do you see? Cut out the coffee!"

The nurse steps into the hall. "Will you come in now?" she asks the father, who twists his hat nervously round and round. "Doctor would like to speak to you." The father nods humbly. First he was afraid for his son. Now he's afraid of the doctor. He goes in. . . .

At five A.M. in the Women's Ward, a very old lady felt rather than saw the first faint flush of the rising sun and imagined how it was touching with rose beauty the wet fields, dark and furrowed. In a little while, perhaps already, her grandson, that tall denimed strength of youth, would be bringing the team out of the barn. The harness would slap on gleaming dappled flanks, the mist curl up from the barnyard, and, "Gee, Pat," the young voice would call in the morning stillness. "Gee, Mac," and the lifted plough, the pulling horses, the strong farm boy who could work from dawn to dusk would move toward the sloping fields. Only, the old lady thought, sometime today they'll interrupt him. "Granny's gone," they'll tell him. He won't be surprised. But he'll be sad. That's good to know. The sun was rising quickly. Yes, he'd be out in the fields by now. The old lady's head sank deeper on the pillow. She welcomed the long-evaded stranger.

At six, the students began to bring the pans around, the wash basins, the thermometers. The students ignored inevitable grumblings. Here or there one younger than the rest would explain they had to get this done before the morning nurses came on, but generally no one bothered. The patients could go back to sleep if they wanted to. If they didn't complain about this, it would be something else, and sleepy nurses, nearing the end of their shift, didn't much care what it was.

At seven, the morning shift came on, heard the reports, what was new and what was gone, took over as the night nurses left for coffee, sleep, or, not rarely, an unwise decision to skip sleep and run into town.

Alonzo, at home, was dunking biscotta in his coffee, and the old lady was already in the morgue. But the hospital functioned.

When Rosemary came into the garden at nine, Dr. Grafton was sitting on the bench beside the goldfish, legs stretched out, hands in the pockets of his blue suit. He jumped up as she approached.

"Well, it's a wonderful day for music," he greeted, wondering why she had that huddled air. As if she protected something inside. But what? Decidedly, there was something in Miss Joplin that shouldn't be there. Dr. Grafton felt sanguine about his ability to draw it out. He was young and intelligent, a little brash, and very sure of himself—the stuff that psychiatrists are made of.

"I phoned my father," Rosemary said as they went down the hill. "He says Mr. Vandebruck will be glad to have us listen. He's practicing till twelve, and then we're invited for lunch, if you like. I have to be back by two-thirty."

"Don't start talking about when you have to get back already. We'll have you here."

"How's Mrs. Parker?" Rosemary asked, wondering if she would ever find another subject of conversation to introduce with Dr. Grafton. She was interested in Mrs. Parker, but surely there must be something else they could talk about? She wished she could think of something. She wished the peculiar hot feeling in her cheeks would go or the headache she'd felt coming on since last night. I'm probably getting a cold, she thought.

"Mrs. Parker's trouble," the doctor was saying, "is too much self-concern and too little self-control. Come to think of it, that's the trouble with a lot of us." Rosemary gave a slight start, but he went on easily enough. "After she realized that her husband was carrying a double load of emotion and disappointment, she was a bit better. It wasn't as if she couldn't have another baby. She's gone home, you know."

"Yes, I heard she had."

"Oh well, they'll be all right in time, I guess. Very nice people." He seemed, not to have lost interest in the Parkers, but to feel that they could safely be left to their own devices now. He's going to be a good doctor, Rosemary thought. He has warmth and intensity, but he knows how to move on. It's when you get locked in emotion that you cease to be a good doctor,

or nurse, or person. Like a bird in a net . . . the sky is all around
him, and he's a bird still, but to no purpose.

Pieter Vandebruck was at the organ when Rosemary and Dr.
Grafton walked softly down the aisle, up the vestry stairs, and
along a little hall to the choir loft. The musician's figure at the
large console looked too slight for mastery, but the great pipes
were his servants; they spoke in his voice. They sang the "Panis
Angelicus," and the low music rang in the vaulted ceiling,
reached into every shadowed corner of the church.

Rosemary leaned against the high-backed bench and received
the music. She was no longer Rosemary. A swelling heart, a listening ear, a spirit swaying on the deep chords . . . but not Rosemary. This was more than beauty. It was release.

At the ruby, the green, the deep blue and yellow windows,
sunlight flashed for entry but spent its brilliance on glowing
casements. Vast and jeweled, the windows seemed hung in
space, the church within kept its dim contours and stretches,
the darkened altar a thing of silence, the empty pews a shadowed awaiting.

There's a strange thing, Dr. Grafton thought, a strange thing
about this music. Vandebruck was a master; all the world knew
that. But what was there in his playing that made the air so . . .
restless? As if he wove a tapestry of music through which a
searching figure moved, eloquent, unanswered. No repose in
this music. Even in the tranquil passages, unrest. This was a
lofty pinnacle, the purest utterance of man, this music. Then
why the searching figure, the reposeless note?

He was playing now (Bach, was it?) something surer, less
somber, and richly colored than the Franck. Yes, Bach. Strong,
clear, triumphant, the music of a sure faith. Dr. Grafton turned
his head a little, trying to recall. . . .

121

"'Rejoice, Beloved Christians,'" Rosemary said. Her lips seemed hardly to move.

Pieter Vandebruck played as though he believed the music but not the message.

They thought he was unaware of them, but presently he rose and waved from the organ gallery to where they sat. Then he disappeared through the loft door.

"He's on his way down," Rosemary said. In silence they descended the vestry stairs to meet Mr. Vandebruck at the church doors. Walking up the aisle, Rosemary gazed at the rose window above the organ loft. As she looked, the window darkened, the deep-glowing colors greyed and went out. A shadow moving over the sun. Rosemary halted, looking up, and in a moment, like a curtain drawn to admit light, the colors reappeared in a dazzling sideways procession across the tracery of the great round window.

"All right," she sighed and moved on. Mr. Vandebruck held the door, and they stepped into the vicarage garden, where the day seemed to snap and sparkle and the air had a scented warmth.

"Rosemary, you are Rosemary," said Mr. Vandebruck, taking both her hands in his. "How very good to meet you at last."

"I . . . it's wonderful, Mr. Vandebruck. Thank you for the very great privilege." No one hearing her could doubt what the music had meant. Mr. Vandebruck was touched. "Ah, so. . . ." He waved a hand. "I'm glad. . . ."

"This is Dr. Grafton, Mr. Vandebruck. Father said you would be pleased to have him come with me."

"So I am, so I am. How do you do, Dr. Grafton?" The little organist peered into the doctor's face. "Doctors especially should listen to music. There is more of the world's harshness in a doctor's ear, do you not think?"

"There's a good deal of it," Dr. Grafton said and added impulsively. "I think you've heard some of its harshness yourself, Mr. Vandebruck?"

They were walking toward the parsonage. Rosemary strayed a little behind. Her headache, forgotten while the music played, seemed to be worse now.

Dr. Vandebruck glanced up at his tall companion. "You heard that in the music?" he asked.

"Well, I heard a sort of . . . restlessness. A lack of peace. Is that what I mean?"

"I think so. Peace. But how to play peacefully now? Bach wrote 'Come, Redeemer,' confident his Redeemer would come. We have no such confidence today. Hope, desire. But not peace, not confidence. This paces my music, I think. This lost peace of Bach's."

He's right, Rosemary thought. She found a measure of peace herself, knowing Pieter Vandebruck couldn't find it.

At the parsonage door, screened now so that the redolent air fused with the musty odor of the hall, Dr. and Mrs. Joplin stood, rather ceremoniously, to greet them. From her vantage behind the two men, Rosemary studied her stepmother, whose long face seemed, as always, to reflect the discomfort of her feet. She looked older than she was, and there seemed, unreasonably, some design in the way she pulled her colorless hair tight back to a skimpy bun, the uninspired looseness of her dress, the lack of rouge on her thin lips. To Rosemary, the woman in the doorway could have been a statue entitled, "Benefits Forgot." Oh, she'd be the one, Rosemary told herself, to chasten the thoughtless, to remind, remind . . . tell us our duty and do hers inflexibly. The stone perfection, reminding us that our feet are clay clear up to our waists. The mood of the music fell away, and Rosemary followed the others into the polished mahogany parlor, where the parson produced some sherry. Rosemary refused, excused herself, and left the room. If she didn't have some aspirin, she'd never get through the meal.

"This isn't very good, doctor," her father apologized, handing a little glass to the young man. "I like to feel the spirit of an occasion excuses even poor wine. 'He that is of merry heart hath a continual feast,'" he added, uncertain as usual whether the quotation fit the time.

"I'm a poor judge, in any case," Dr. Grafton said. "Of wine, I mean. But I'm very glad to be here, and it's been an honor to hear Mr. Vandebruck."

"I'm glad of an audience, as my friend here knows," Mr. Vandebruck protested. "More especially of an audience with so keen an ear as yours. Yes, yes, do not shake your head. It takes the good ear to find the performer's question under the master's music. I would be happy to have you attend a recital tonight, tomorrow, if you have time and would care to?"

"I'd like nothing better. It's too late to do anything tonight, but I think I could get someone to take over tomorrow for me. I'm certainly going to try."

"Ah, good, I shall look for you." He turned to Dr. Joplin. "Charles, I have not said how beautiful your young one is. You and Ruth must be very proud."

Dr. Joplin smiled, but Mrs. Joplin rose abruptly. "I must see to lunch," she explained.

Surprised at her reaction, Dr. Grafton watched the woman leave the room. Her feet fell heavily, and there was a burdened sag to her whole body. Flat feet, the doctor thought. But something else is flat here. Not Mr. Vandebruck. This family of three. They all seem ironed out in each other's presence. He wondered what Dr. and Mrs. Joplin were like when Rosemary wasn't in the house. His eye caught Mr. Vandebruck's, and they each looked quickly away, but not before a frown of speculation had passed between them. Then the organist, too, found something afflicted in this rather pleasantly old-fashioned parlor.

At lunch, a meal of cheese soufflé, mushrooms, little new peas, watermelon pickle, biscuits, and lemon pie that Dr. Grafton relished to the last mouthful, Mr. Vandebruck reminisced upon the world of music. Dr. Joplin spoke little, dividing his attention between his wife and Rosemary. Rather, Dr. Grafton thought, like a man who hopes by the power of his eyes to keep a pair of antagonists apart. Well, it was clear enough that Mrs. Joplin and her daughter were unsympathetic. Which would account for a good deal, the doctor thought. I knew there was something troubling that girl. It could be resentment of her stepmother. Resentment's bad. It's a debilitating, exclusive emotion, and it nourishes itself. He thought Mrs. Joplin's attitude more complicated. She looked at once obstinate and understanding, puzzled and wise. She looked tired but strong.

I wonder, he thought, what the first Mrs. Joplin was like.

On the streetcar, going back to the hospital, Rosemary began to wonder if she'd be able to go on duty at all. Her head was racketing with pain, and the hot flush in her cheeks had increased. You'd think, she reflected bitterly, that Aesculapius here would notice something. I'd probably have to fold in six sections at his feet before he'd think to wonder why I've barely said a word since noon. Flu, I bet. I'm probably getting the flu.

At that, Dr. Grafton, who had been studying her with concern since they left the church, reached over and took her hand. It was hot and dry. Her eyes, when she glanced his way, were much too bright, the lids heavy.

"I think when we get back you'd better trot over to the Infirmary. Where they'll probably keep you. Did you feel like this this morning?"

Rosemary shook her head miserably. "No. Not really. I had a sort of headache, but I wanted to hear Vandebruck. I thought a couple of aspirin would fix me up. It'll take more than aspirin, doctor," she added a little wildly, her voice rising. "Maybe you can figure it out . . . I can't."

The passengers had turned to stare, than averted their eyes from the young girl making a spectacle of herself. Dr. Grafton took no notice of them at all. He was trying to think how best to get her to the Infirmary. Get off and call a cab, or ride the few remaining blocks to the streetcar stop? He was stunned for a moment at the effect of her sudden fever.

"Come along, Rosemary," he said. "We're going to get out and take a taxi."

"Taxi?" she muttered, stumbling against his supporting arm. But she went along unprotesting.

In the cab, she slumped against him, tipping her head back to stare at him with brilliant eyes. "Did you know you called me Rosemary? What's your name?"

"It's Kenneth."

"Kenneth. How stylish. What do you think, Kenneth, of that monument of tact and goodness, my stepmother?" Her head fell against his shoulder as she whispered, "You should have seen my mother. She called me Rosemarie."

At the hospital, they bundled her onto a stretcher and off to the Nurses' Infirmary. When she'd gone, Dr. Grafton stood a moment, staring at the closed elevator doors. Then he shoved his hands in his pockets and walked slowly to his room, where he found doctors Horner and Dolphin, fellow interns. From his phonograph, turned low, the flashing fingers of Meade Lux Lewis boogied a crawl.

"Hi, Ken. You don't mind, do you?" Dr. Dolphin asked from the bed where he was stretched, arms behind his head. "You have to pay the penalty for owning the only phonograph in the place. Picked this platter up downtown, and we wanted to hear it before we went back on."

"OK, Dolph. Any time."

Kenneth listened in silence till the record finished, wondering if Vandebruck liked boogie. Personally, he couldn't stand it, but some of the big fellows had catholic tastes. After these two left, he thought he'd take a nap. That girl was really very upsetting.

"Sent," said Dolph, removing the record. "I'm truly sent."

"It's all right," Horner agreed. "I like old-fashioned stuff better. Victor Herbert."

"Never heard of him," said Dolph proudly. "What's biscotta? Either of you guys know?"

"Some sort of Italian biscuit, I think. Very hard," Grafton answered. "They dunk it."

"Had a kid come in this morning with acute indigestion. Seems he eats biscotta and coffee three times a day. I tried to scare him into a few proteins and vitamins, but I'll bet my socks he's dunking this minute. Oh well. Speaking of which, I think I'll mush over for some coffee myself. Anyone coming?"

"I'm on," Horner said. "Only it'll have to be a short one. How about it, Ken?"

"Nope, thanks. I'm going to curl on my rumpled bed and get some sleep."

"Didn't I see you go off with one of the nurses this morning? The girl with the flaxen hair?" Dolph asked.

"You did."

"Tch, tch. That's no way to further your career, my boy. Or has she got a rich papa who believes in independent females?"

"No rich papa. A minister," Ken answered shortly. Dolph's theories about interns and wealthy girls were pretty dull. "You go to too many movies."

"*Oh, I wanna be a doctor like Dr. Kildare,*" Dolph sang. In spite of themselves, the others smiled. "Where'd you go anyway? Or is it none of my business. Just curious about the hour, you know."

"We heard Pieter Vandebruck play."

Dr. Dolphin wrinkled his nose. "Organ, isn't he?"

"Yes. It was very—stirring," Kenneth said, and then felt as though he'd betrayed Vandebruck.

"Maybe so. Haven't heard the organ in years, but as I recall the only thing it stirred in me was an ardent desire for a more comfortable seat."

"Fascinating, these glimpses of your past. Say, could either of you take over for me tomorrow night?" Kenneth asked as they headed for the door. Horner and Dolph exchanged glances.

"I suppose I could. . . ." Dolph said slowly.

"You sound like Horatio saying *I'll* defend the bridge! I'll take one of your nights, so what have you got to lose?"

"Well, natch. You don't think I'm doing it for free. Is it Goldie again?"

"Miss Joplin's in the Infirmary," Kenneth said with great stiffness and immediately felt like a fool.

"Doesn't surprise me at all," Dolph said. "She ought to get massive doses of liver extract. That sort of pale blonde needs a lot of vitality to bring out her looks. Said to myself when I saw her this morning that the girl was. . . ."

"It'll pay off," Grafton interrupted, "this ability of yours to diagnose on the run." I'm losing my sense of humor, he thought irritably. "I don't get enough sleep," he decided aloud.

"Who does?" Dolph shrugged. "OK. I'll pull your chestnuts and you pull mine." He and Horner left, Dolph busily explaining to Horner, who'd heard it before, that he never started dating girls in the summer. "Any girl," he said, "can look good in the summer. You can't tell one cotton from the next. But in the winter, . . . Ah. It's when the mutation minks come out that I get on the qui vivre."

"You better get on it now," Horner replied, "or we won't get on the floor."

Dr. Grafton dropped to the bed, pulled off his shoes, stretched out. Dolph, tireless, tiresome, was a pretty good doctor nevertheless, and though he was liable to talk your ears off, he was pretty sure to counter by giving you his shirt.

He closed his eyes. Fatigued in every bone, he was. Hadn't been to bed in more hours than he could count. But it hadn't seemed a good idea to tell Rosemary he was on night duty now. Rosemary. Poor little thing, she's really in a tangle, he thought. He felt the tingly stirring within that always occurred when he'd found a psychological problem . . . the dark emotion, a foe skulking in the brain.

The following evening, in the now-crowded church, Kenneth on a side-aisle seat leaned back, as well as anyone can in a pew, and tried to listen wholeheartedly to the music. He hadn't had yesterday and never, he judged, would have the utter absorption Rosemary had showed. Such a loss of identity in music was like a flight from life, and Dr. Grafton was entirely too concerned with life to flee it even briefly. She had been in an enchantment, he thought. A sort of death. Now, though the splendid harmonies rolled over him, he couldn't keep from thinking of the girl who'd been here yesterday.

"Move over, willya?" The question was twice repeated, in a hushed hurried voice, before Dr. Grafton realized that it was intended for him. He turned to face a frowning brown-thatched boy, about twelve.

"Huh?" said Dr. Grafton densely.

"Over, over," the boy whispered impatiently.

Dr. Grafton turned toward his neighbor, observed a small space between them, edged over. The resulting bit of bare pew adequately accommodated the newcomer.

"Thanks," that one whispered, then slumped in reverent attention. "Beautiful," he said at the conclusion of the prelude to Saint-Saens' "*Deluge.*" He sighed, shaking his head as though unable to believe his ears. He turned to Dr. Grafton. "Thanks for shoving over. Lemme see your program, please?" Silently the doctor handed over the program, and the young music lover brooded on it, handed it back with another, "Thanks."

"That's perfectly all right," the doctor assured him. "I guess you really like music," he went on, sounding somewhat fatuous to himself and apparently to the boy, who lifted his brows in a disconcertingly adult fashion. "I heard Mr. Vandebruck practice yesterday," Kenneth said in an effort to readjust their positions. This was successful, for the boy looked dazzled with awe.

"Gosh," he said enviously. "Well, anyway, I got here tonight. Rest of the kids are practicing."

"Music?"

"Nah. A play. I'm in it too, but Mrs. Joplin told me I could skip it tonight and come hear Vandebruck."

"What's the play?"

" 'Foam Maiden.' It's an old Celtic folk piece. I'm Michael, who holds a merrow in thrall," he went on with utter lack of emphasis.

"Who are you, really?"

"Aaron Ross. Who're you?"

"Kenneth Grafton."

"How do you do."

"How do you do."

Aaron fluttered a hand for silence as the organist resumed his place. During the performance of a Bach choral prelude, Dr. Grafton studied the young person beside him. Not by the movement of a muscle did the boy acknowledge any interest save in the music. He consented, however, to speak between numbers.

"Mrs. Joplin?" he said, in answer to a question of Kenneth's. "She's directing the play. She always does."

"Very nice person," Kenneth said, disliking himself, but driven by what he considered an urgency greater than the display of good taste.

"Sure she is." The canny Aaron fell thoughtlessly into the trap, perhaps because the conversation struck him as a little silly.

"You know her daughter, Rosemary?"

"Miss Joplin? Sure, I know her." The tone of his voice announced his opinion of Miss Joplin. "Of course," he added grudgingly, "she does like music."

"How did you know?"

"See her at concerts in New York. My pop takes me. I play piano and oboe."

"That's quite a program, with play acting too."

"Oh, that. I only do it to please Mrs. Joplin. She gets a bang out of putting on productions."

"Does Miss Joplin go to the plays?"

"Her?" The boy laughed a little. "Not on your life. I saw her peeking in at us the other day. You know, she's got the mopiest face I ever did see."

"What's a merrow?" Kenneth asked abruptly.

But Master Ross had sunk into silence again at the first clear singing note of the organ.

The recital over, Kenneth lost Aaron in the audience exodus. Mr. Vandebruck was at the great open doors, shaking many hands and saying I'm so glad, but when he saw Kenneth, he extricated himself and hurried over.

"Ah, doctor. How terrible this is about Rosemary. How does she find herself tonight?"

"I called before I left. She still has a high temperature, and they wouldn't let me see her. But I'll be able to tomorrow. I'll give Mrs. . . . . uh, Dr. Joplin, a ring."

Mr. Vandebruck pursed his lips thoughtfully but said only, "Will you have time to come to the house? A small reception, I believe. . . ."

"I'd like to very much. But if you could wait just a second, and I could find. . . ." He craned his neck over the crowds. "Oh yes, there he is. . . . If you would come with me for just a moment, Mr. Vandebruck, I'd like to introduce you to one of your deepest admirers," he said as they weaved through the throng. "Here we are. . . . Mr. Vandebruck, this is Aaron Ross."

"Sir," said Aaron, after an admiring glance at Kenneth from whom he had expected nothing like this, "Sir, this is an honor. . . ."

Chapter 12.

"HAVE you been up to see Rosemary yet?" Gretchen asked, setting her tray on the table and pulling up a chair next to Nelle's.

"Just going. My mother's coming over."

"Oh, good." Gretchen sorted out various plates with her usual dining-room expression of surprised indignation, sat down. "Have a good time with Wally the other day?" she inquired around a mouthful of what seemed to be fresh ham but might possibly be veal. "What is this?"

Nelle, who in the course of a few days had shifted her sights from the point where Wally was "Gretchen's Wally" to the position of being unable to endure Gretchen's so much as mentioning him, answered only the second part of the question. "Veal, I suppose. That's what I'm considering it."

"I asked if you had a good time with Wally," Gretchen repeated.

"Very. We went to the Egyptian room of the Museum."

"Oh, murder."

Gretchen, who had many excellent qualities, did not number subtlety among them. Her comments were not in the least malicious. It was obvious to her that Wally had been her friend for ages and that she had more or less sponsored Nelle for him. What could be more natural than an active interest in the progress of their relationship? She said "oh murder" in good faith, went on eating, and was completely astounded to hear Nelle demand in a truculent tone, "What do you mean, oh murder?"

"What? Oh, I just meant it's so sort of stuffy. Don't you see enough corpses around here?" At that point, she decided to back water, though quite conscious of her own probity, because, lacking subtlety, she was still perfectly able to recognize outrage when brought face to face with it. "Oh, I do think he's loads of fun," she said heartily. "And whatever else you have to say about him, Wally is certainly attentive. All that dashing around to open doors and everything." She pushed aside some turnips with a sigh. On reflection, the waters into which she backed seemed rather troubled.

"What time will your mother be here?" she asked.

Nelle muttered some time or other, and then, because she could never quite resist Gretchen's rather overpowering good humor, said why didn't they meet and go up to Rosemary together. "If they'll let us all in at once."

"Oh, well, I don't suppose they will. But I'd like to see your mother. You leaving?"

"Yes. I have a few things. . . ." Nelle backed off, the sentence unfinished, and walked jerkily away.

She really should practice walking with a book on her head, Gretchen thought. People never do seem to realize how important the back of them is. She went to the counter for ice cream, returned to her seat, sat for a while tapping a spoon on the table top until a neighbor eyed her with enough significance to halt the spoon in mid-air. My word, what a lot of neurotics, Gretchen observed to herself. There's Rosemary, as delicately balanced as a cat. And Nelle certainly gets a bit thin-lipped when she's miffed. That square healthy sort of girl should never let herself look offended. And there's this character over here going all to pieces because of a little spoon. Gretchen, whose own nerves were well controlled, looked faintly troubled. And then, with no decision, she was thinking of Dr. Whitney. The thought was like a strong salt sea breeze, whisking away the floppy irritations around her. He was no neurotic. He was clean and uncluttered as a new nail. But more than that, he had arrived at a dignified understanding with life, not asking too much of it but firm about his rights. He and his father seemed very much alike.

She got up to collect the dishes, wondering, with the nearest thing to wistfulness possible for her, whether they'd ever ask her to tea again.

Mrs. Gibson arrived half an hour later in a taxi. She wore a silk print dress, a flung scarf of mink with little bright-eyed faces snapping here and there in the silky fur, a hat of pink and blue and yellow sweet peas. "Utter extravagance," she told Gretchen. "It's a one-day hat, a one-afternoon hat, really. I thought it might cheer Rosemary. And I bought her the most divine little nightie you ever saw . . . there you are, dear," she said as Nelle came in, "Do straighten up, and can we see Rosemary immediately? Whatever in the world is the matter? Influenza? But isn't that something science has conquered?"

Rosemary lay, not at all unaware of where she was or what was wrong. Only it was easier just to keep her eyes closed and not notice when people said how are you, or how is she, if they really thought she slept. There seemed to be an awful lot of moving around in the room, and she wondered if it always seemed so to patients, if the voices buzzed faintly, grew louder, came and went in this incessant mesh of meaningless syllables.

Eyes closed, she could separate the sounds . . . opening or closing of the door, which was really not a sound at all but a movement of air; flat clink of the glass straw in the glass tumbler; rush of water in the adjoining bathroom. Outside and below, the distant voices of people going to and from the hospital; near by, voices of birds flickering through leaves and branches. Eyes closed, she seemed to be in a swirling greyness, like moor mist in movies about Englishmen being murdered, in a pearl fog that moved and rolled on itself.

Now, for a while, there had been silence. The sort of silence that even a person with her eyes closed would know for emptiness. There was no one in the room. Ice stirred in the glass tumbler, but that was its own cool melting. Something went past the door with a swish and a little thud. That would be the porter sweeping the hall, bumping his broom softly against the walls.

She opened her eyes. Yes, quite empty. Just outside the window a blue jay swung impudently on an oak twig. His black eyes glittered with a pert braininess, seeming to look into hers. A blue jay, she thought, is the only bird that looks intelligent. This one was simply bursting with knavish intentions. He cocked his little hooded head, flashed past her and away. The twig swayed slower and slower and became still.

On the table beside her, a blue hyacinth in a brown pot breathed fragrance from every thick curled petal. The hyacinth looked like a little church door. There was a card propped against the pot, and she pushed her head around on the pillow to read "Preston," in a graceful hand. How nice of him, she thought. How very very nice. She hadn't heard him come in. Probably he hadn't. Being Preston, he would find the most perfect hyacinth in the greenhouse and realize that it could speak his message best. He'd give it to a nurse then, to take up.

She had thought for a moment it would be so easy to lie wide-eyed, considering this and that in a leisurely way. But heavily her lids came down. The effort to lift them was quite beyond her. It's the pill, she thought slowly. What was it Virginia Woolf wrote? *"That great prince with the moth's eyes and the feathered feet, one of whose names is Chloral."* There was the grey mist again, and there, coming toward her, murmuring, was sleep. . . .

Mrs. Gibson and Gretchen murmured into the room. By special permission and only for a minute.

"Oh dear, she's asleep," Nelle's mother whispered. "Let's not disturb her. Here, I'll put the little nightie where she can find it when she wakes." She lay the silver-speckled, white-ribboned, delicate package on the table beside the hyacinth and tiptoed away.

Faintly, Rosemary heard them come and go. But her eyes were heavy, her voice lost in some smothered place, and she wanted only to lie still—like, she thought duskily, like a fairy-tale princess, enchantedly asleep. In fairy tales, the stepmother is always wicked, always punished. When Rosemary had been a child, she'd loved the fairy tales. She'd never minded the cruelty, the savage reprisals, the unearned benefits. How right they'd seemed—the diamond mountains, gold-treed forests, underground rivers, and jeweled nightingales. How right that good should be beautiful, simpleness rewarded.

She dreamed of her mother. . . .

There was the mist again, rolling on itself, and through it, murmuring, came a hooded procession, streaming from a little church door up a hill toward Rosemary. Though the hill was low and empty, the ribbon of figures wound and wound. Rosemary, at the summit, thought, they'll never get here. Weaving, the line came toward her, but so slowly she thought they'd never reach her. And if they do, she thought, I can run. And then they were upon her and all around her and of course she couldn't run. She was in the middle, and beside her was a deep hole, and on the other side of the hole was a glass coffin. The mist swirled, but her mother was in the coffin, and Rosemary could see her. Then the grey people moved up and strung the coffin with ribbons and lowered it into the hole. Rosemary leaned over and over, watching as it went down. "Good-by," she called in a clear voice. "Good-by, Mother." Her mother lifted a hand in a small gesture, and "Good-by," her thin call came back. "Rosemarie—*forgive me.*"

The scream welled up, dashing her eyes open as it cried into the room. Then she lay back against the pillows, the breath rushing into her lungs, her eyes traveling rapidly around the room, as though to be sure of it.

Kenneth was sitting in a chair by the window, watching her. He smiled when she saw him, just enough of a smile to say, "Well here I am, and I'm going to be a help to you." He didn't say anything at all for a while, but finding him there as she came out of the gulf of nightmare gave her unexpected courage. So much that she in a moment was able to smile a little too and say with a touch of challenge, "I suppose very few analysts are ever around while the dream actually takes place."

"Oh, very few. I'm lucky." He leaned back with a leisured, comforting attitude, as though his time were all at her disposal. "Think you could tell me about it?" he asked.

Mrs. Gibson offered to treat the girls to a soda in the Coffee Shop. When Bitsy saw them coming, she decided immediately that this elegant woman, looking like a morning in Elizabeth Arden's, must be Miss Bemis' mother. She took their order, two sodas and a black coffee, then narrowed her eyes to examine the sweet-pea hat.

"It's real!" she blurted. "Oh, 'scuse me. I was just sort of surprised."

"That's all right," Mrs. Gibson assured her. "You mean it doesn't look real?"

"Tell you the truth, ma'am, it don't. I thought it was real good imitations. But that's a pretty idea all right. You think of it yourself?" Bitsy, as more than one had remarked, had no natural sense of social barriers. Give her a friendly person like Mrs. Gibson, and she'd stand there with a tray on her hip, a wad of gum dancing between her jaws, and talk till the snow flew.

"Well, yes, I did. At least, I suppose other people have thought of it too, but so did I. Such a disappointment to find they don't *look* real."

"Oh now," Bitsy comforted, "they do when you get close. And anyway," she leaned over ever so slightly to sniff, "anyway, it's probably like real pearls. You know, even if no one else does. Guess I better pop; old Howie there is giving me the high sign. Back in a jiff. Two black and whites and one coffee black, right?" She ambled off, showing Howie the counter man that she might obey orders but wouldn't break her neck doing it.

"Well," said Mrs. Gibson when their drinks were at last before them and Bitsy was not. "I'll come again in a few days. Rosemary *should* be better in a few days?" Nelle and Gretchen assured her that was so, and she went on, a little relieved at being out of the atmosphere of a sick room. Mrs. Gibson felt uncomfortable with emotional stress, preferring to skim placidly along a neutral stream of feeling where demands on the mind and heart were, on the whole, pleasant and easily satisfied. "I must rush in a bit. I have to send a basket of fruit to the Townsends. They're going abroad, fortunate ones," she said mendaciously. She herself had been abroad twice and wouldn't consider going further than Martha's Vineyard again in her life. She wouldn't be in the Townsend's shoes for anything but was delighted to send them a large basket and a small note.

She looked around the Coffee Shop with interest. At, particularly, two young interns laughing at the counter. My word, she thought, have those two been here all the time? When I was a girl. . . . Neither Gretchen nor Nelle seemed at all aware of the young men. It was curious. Of course, in Gretchen's case, she probably had too much to think about already in the way of admirers. But Nelle, now. Could it be, she wondered uncomfortably, sour grapes? Possibly one could develop a taste for them—like olives. She glanced at her daughter and felt a sudden admiration for her. Really, it was rather admirable that the girls of today had such a straightforward acceptance of themselves, recognizing their own faults and assets and proceeding on the premise that, if flirtation closed its doors, others were open. Then too, she went on, sipping her coffee, when I was a girl, there simply were not many doors open. The girls I knew had no need to work and no encouragement to think, so we flirted and got married or flirted and got left. It's much better this way. She thought, for the first time, that Nelle had showed very good sense in refusing Miss Worcester's, where the pattern undoubtedly remained much the same as it had been twenty-five years ago and was not a pattern into which Nelle could have gracefully fitted herself. Besides, she reminded herself pleasantly, it appears now that Wally Chase is really interested, and he'd have been a feather in any cap I knew. Rather testily, she felt that he produced only the superficialities of his conversation for her, but that wasn't really too important.

"Your Aunt May," she said, flicking open her doeskin bag to rummage for change, "is sending a copy of the 'Rubaiyat.'"

"Sending it where?" Nelle asked.

"To the Townsends."

Nelle stared. "You mean she's sending them the 'Rubaiyat' as a bon-voyage present?"

Mrs. Gibson nodded. "She made it all herself out of parchment and illuminated letters, like the monks. Only I don't suppose it's really parchment because that's the skin of baby animals, isn't it? Well, something that's crackly and used looking like parchment. She painted pictures too. I don't think your Aunt is a very good painter."

Nelle continued incredulous. Gretchen laughed. "Oh well," she observed, "everybody has to get at least one beautifully illustrated copy of the 'Rubaiyat' during his lifetime. It won't take up much room."

"Oh, but it's simply enormous," Mrs. Gibson protested. "May says all the manuscripts copied by the monks were. At least two feet high. She copied it all in old English with a quill pen and decorative borders."

"They'll pitch it overboard," Nelle warned.

"Oh, dear. I did try to tell May. But telling May is so difficult."

"Don't I know it," Nelle mourned, thinking of the oil hanging in her room. "Well, it's the Townsend's problem, not ours. Speaking of going abroad, Wally is going to Rome this fall to look at The Ceiling."

"I should think he'd go to Cheops and look at the floor," Gretchen murmured.

"Cheops," said Nelle, from the wealth of lately acquired information, "was the king, called Khufu, of Egypt. He was not a place." She delivered this intelligence with a blasé air that caused her mother to glance quickly at Gretchen, who remained unruffled and said she never had been able to figure out Pharaohs.

"Wally has a friend who climbed the scaffolding when they repaired The Ceiling," Nelle went on with happy smugness.

"Really?" Gretchen's interest was captured now. "How amazing. What part was he near?"

"The Deluge. All those people trying to get out of the water in a heap, you know."

Gretchen did know, from pictures and reproductions. She

had to smile at how like her mother Nelle sounded now and then, though no doubt both would be astonished to hear it. "If I could climb the scaffolding, and had my choice," she mused, "I'd pick Isaiah. He's the best of the prophets. Michelangelo's best, I mean." She thought of the power and reposeful wisdom of Isaiah, the grave, knowing eyes, the beautiful acute mouth. *He looks just like Dr. Whitney*, she thought with innocent directness. "Wally never told me about that," she said.

Nelle's smiling lack of response spoke loudly. *Of course*, her mother thought, *it's obvious that Gretchen doesn't pine at all for Wally, but she has the most gracious way of building Nelle's ego without seeming to.*

"I'm perfectly sure," she said warmly, "that you'll get to Italy some day, Gretchen."

"Oh, but I'm not interested really. It's not likely they'll be repairing the ceiling of the Sistine Chapel again in my lifetime, and anyway I think you can get a better view by looking at good reproductions. At least, that's what everyone who's been over there tells me. I wouldn't make a very good traveler. Not even to Italy."

"Ah, Fiorenzo," Mrs. Gibson sighed automatically.

"You've been there, I guess," Gretchen said.

"Oh, yes. I was all over Italy." She didn't add that at the time it had felt as though Italy were all over her. That might very well offend Nelle, who was beginning to be quite possessive about ancient grounds. "Archer and I went off for a perfect idyll in Capri," she added, dutifully bringing in all she could remember of the trip, since it was unlikely she'd be talking about Italy again for ages.

Gretchen, thinking of Mr. Gibson, not conceivably the sort of man to take along on an idyll, struggled for composure. "Oh, golly," she said finally, hoping it would seem to apply to inner thoughts. But Mrs. Gibson said, "I know," in a voice that hovered over a laugh. Nelle, still thinking contentedly that after all Wally couldn't have been too fond of Gretchen, since he never told her much of anything, didn't notice.

"You know," Mrs. Gibson said now, "I believe I'll give a dinner party. A graduation dinner. Don't you think that would be fun?"

"Oh, that'd be marvelous." Nelle and Gretchen shared the answer.

"I just thought of it this very minute. The day after graduation, I think. Because I suppose it would be too exhausting for everybody to have it the same evening. Will your dear parents be here, Gretchen?"

"Not Dad, but Mom's coming."

"Oh? Not your father? What a disappointment."

"Too far for Dad. He says it's because he can't leave the shop. But I know Dad. Just the thought of a trip sends him panting to the hammock."

"Is that so? He must be a restful sort of person."

"You could call him that," Gretchen agreed.

"Well now, let's see. . . . You, your mother, Nelle and, uh. . . ."

"Nelle and Wally," Gretchen supplied soberly.

"Yes. Nelle and Wally. Rosemary. . . . Do you think Rosemary will be all right?"

"Oh, heavens, yes. She'll be fine long before that, I should think."

"Wonderful. . . . Now, who is there she'd like to have?"

"Apparently," said Nelle, "she's snagged an intern. That Grafton you were telling me about, Gretchen."

Gretchen ran a spoon around the inside of her glass, getting the froth up. "Do you think it was snagging? I mean, it seems to me more another case of Dr. Grafton's urge to balance people."

143

"Balance?" Mrs. Gibson repeated. "Rosemary isn't. . . ."

"Of course not," Gretchen interrupted. "But she's upset. He adores upsets. Correcting them, that is."

"Is he a psychoanalyst?"

"Oh no, not yet. It takes ages. But you can always spot them early, the ones who are really interested in it. And another thing, when they are gone on the subject of the psyche, they hardly notice anything else. So how could he get snagged? It takes a little cooperation on both sides, you know."

"Maybe you're right," Nelle agreed. "Actually, I imagine Rosemary is . . . well, what do I mean? Not too interested in herself, but. . . ."

"Too much on her mind," Gretchen interpreted.

"I suppose she has," Nelle said. "But there's one thing sure, if Dr. Grafton's really interested in her, he'll go to any lengths to help her. Everyone says he's marvelous." She finished up her soda and sat back. "What were we talking about? Before Rosemary. . . ."

"My dinner party," her mother said. "All right then, we'll ask Dr. Grafton. Now, how about Rosemary's parents? I'd like to make this a sort of family thing, too, since Archer and your mother and I will be there."

Gretchen turned out her hands. "I don't know, really. Rosemary goes home all the time, but. . . ."

"Then I shall simply invite them. The courteous thing cannot be wrong," she said with the confidence of a woman whose criteria are based solely upon social standards. "And you, Gretchen. Is there anyone you'd like?"

Briefly, not seriously, Gretchen considered Dr. Whitney. Only of course she wouldn't ask him. Dr. Whitney was entirely too reserved, to say nothing of too busy, for a dinner invitation to the home of people he didn't know by a girl he had been kind enough to take to tea once. It would be just presumptuous to ask him. "No, thanks," she said. "I'll take Mom. I haven't seen her in so long it will be like having a beau along."

It wasn't till later she realized that there were about half a dozen men scattered here and there, any one of whom she might have suggested, none of whom had occurred to her. I do believe, she thought, that I'm about to give up the field and concentrate. She remembered suddenly something she hadn't thought of in a long time. Why, I entered training to find myself a doctor, she said, shaping each word in her mind, like a conversation. I did, and I'd forgotten. Overcome with unfamiliar shyness, she sat very still, feeling her heart hurry.

But that was later. Now she simply said she'd take her mother and who else would there be?

"I think that would be all. We want to keep it small, and just people who more or less know each other, though actually of course they don't, but you see what I mean. That would be, let's see, ten of us. It's unbalanced, an extra woman. But I can never feel that it really matters, can you?"

"Not a bit, to me" Gretchen said. "We don't have a formal family."

"Neither do we," said Mrs. Gibson, who could be as formal as an ambassador's reception but preferred not to. "Well, I shall ask Mr. Hartwig to come . . . that's Corinna's uncle, the retired seaman," she explained to Gretchen. "He served for us a few weeks ago, because it's just too much for Corinna to cook and serve too." The recollection of Mr. Hartwig's service brought a brooding expression to her face, but she put the thought aside. "I'm so glad I thought of this. . . . I do have to trot now. The Townsends. Oh, and perhaps a few grapes for Rosemary. Doesn't she seem the sort of girl for grapes? I remember reading once about a queen who ate nothing but white grapes at the table, and everyone was marvelously impressed . . . so spirituelle. But she simply gorged in private. Not a very nice story, it certainly wasn't Rosemary who made me think of it, just the grapes. Possibly pears would be better."

As they left, Mrs. Gibson turned to send a smile of farewell to Bitsy, who said she just knew Miss Bemis would have a mother like that.

"What d'y mean?" said Howie. "That's Gibson's mother."

"How come you know so much?"

"I heard her, is all. Gibson called her 'mother' at least six times. And Bemis called her Mrs. Gibson. So?"

"Oh, go boil your head," said Bitsy. She had quite a stock of these admonitory phrases and used them constantly.

Chapter 13.

GRETCHEN rolled her bathing suit and cap in a towel, debating, as she generally did when faced with the task of fitting all her hair into a rubber helmet, whether it wouldn't be better to lop it off. She decided not to, tucked the bundle under her arm and left the room.

Dorry Palmer was in the hall, beautifully groomed and indecisive. In other words, quite herself. Miss Merkle had her ticketed as unreliable in any but the most normal situation, but the girls had elected her chairman of the dance committee because she always seemed to know what to do. She'd managed it nicely, by asking everyone else what ought to be done and then doing whatever most of them advised.

Until Gretchen stepped into the hall, Dorry had been wavering at her door, trying to arrange an afternoon off when nobody else seemed to be around. She brightened at the sight of the one girl whom it was absolutely safe to follow. "Hi, Gretchen," she called. "You going over to the Y?"

"Yes," said Gretchen thinking it was remarkable how Dorry always looked exactly the same—like something enameled.

"Wait for me? I was just thinking I'd like a swim."

"Oh sure." Gretchen strolled into Dorry's room. "I should

think you'd be down getting things ready for that dance tonight."

"Oh, do you think so?" Dorry turned from the closet, bathing suit trailing. "Of course, I was going to in a little while. Everything's done really. Except for last-minute touches. Preston's going to hang the lanterns, only he can't till later, and I thought probably I could wait."

"You know best. I'm not going to stay long at the Y anyway. It occurred to me I ought to start studying for the State Boards."

"So soon?" Dorry said in surprise. "Well, I guess it would be a good idea."

"Lanterns after all, eh?" Gretchen said as they walked down the hall.

"Yes. Isn't that all right? I mean, you can't go wrong with Japanese lanterns. Everybody likes them."

"I don't."

Dorry looked so dismayed that Gretchen added benevolently, "That's nothing to worry about. I suppose most people do. What are the refreshments?"

"I got a caterer," Dorry said happily. "There was enough money, if we used the lanterns again, so anyway the food will be better than last time."

"That's good," Gretchen approved.

Downstairs there was a crowd of students and nurses clustered at the Bulletin Board.

"Let's go see what that is," Gretchen said curiously. She glanced easily over the thronging heads. Everything had been removed from the bulletin but a poster headed United States Army Nurse Corps.

"What is it?" Dorry squealed, hopping up and down. "Oh lordy, I wish I were tall."

"Hold on a sec," Gretchen told her.

148

Around them the buzz of excited young voices filled the lobby and conveyed, in snatches, the text of the notice to Dorry.

"Reserve Corps, it says, what does that mean?"

"Well, read it. Reserve Corps, just what it says."

"I mean, isn't that the one you join but don't do battle?"

"You join, and then if they have to increase the size of the Nurse Corps, they call up some from every hospital."

"That's the idea . . . not pulling the whole staff out of one place. . . ."

"They could hardly do that."

"They can do anything."

Dorry looked up at Gretchen with bright eyes. "What do you think?" she asked.

Gretchen turned from the notice to Dorry. "Think? That they have to do it, of course."

"I mean . . . oh well, for yourself. . . ."

"Good heavens, I can't decide what I think of anything on such short notice."

"Oh, of course not," Dorry agreed. But she listened eagerly to the conversation around her.

"Well, I think it'd be fun," said a graduate of last year. "I'd like to get called right up. At least it'd be something to do."

"Don't you do enough now?" Gretchen asked.

"Oh yes, but not *exciting*, is what I mean. If something exciting doesn't happen to me soon, I'm going to start answering Personals in the paper."

"You be careful," Gretchen said absently, "You'll wind up in a trunk."

"That's for me," said one of the seniors.

"A trunk?" said Dorry.

"Oh, don't be a goon. I'm going right over to Merkle and see

149

how you get into this thing. Do you *have* to stay in the Reserve, Gretchen? Can't you just join the Army?"

Gretchen moved away a little. "I think they're taking volunteers. But don't go by me. Ask Miss Merkle."

Dorry, cocking her head from side to side to glean the majority reaction, noticed Gretchen edging off. "Hey, wait," she called, and hurried after. "Gosh, it's really exciting, isn't it?" She pattered alongside, out of the Residence and across the square to the Y building. She was still contemplating the effect of the notice in a gay voice as they showered and went down from the locker room to the pool. "And they've really tricked up the uniforms no end, Gretchen. You'd look marvelous in them. I think maybe I would too, though we're awfully different. In looks, I mean. . . ."

I hope that's not all, Gretchen thought, suppressing a sigh. She remembered a little woodpecker she'd seen a few days ago, clinging to a tree trunk and slamming away at a hole. He'd been trim and pretty, and Gretchen had decided, watching the rythmic rapping of his mad little head, that there simply couldn't be a thing in there. No brain could take such a battering.

There was no one else at the pool. Green and pungently chlorined it lay before them, every tile visible in the clear still water. Gretchen mounted to the diving board, moved forward three steps, and with a neat little spring launched herself in a smooth arc, up, over, sliding into the cool refuge and swimming down the pool. At the end of four lengths, Dorry called out, "Stop, Gretchen, stop!"

"Huh?" said Gretchen, finally hearing. She swam to the side where Dorry was clinging. "You drowning?"

"Gretchen, it just isn't fair of you to go swimming up and down that way."

"But I came here to swim."

"Every minute?" Dorry sounded outraged.

"What would you suggest?"

"You could talk a minute, couldn't you?"

Gretchen leaned on her arm and laughed till Dorry's hurt expression brought her up short. "I'm sorry. Honestly, though, this is about the only exercise I get. We've been talking for ages, and we can talk some more when we leave, can't we?"

"Oh, I suppose so," Dorry grumbled. She began to giggle herself. "Really, Gretchen, you do look funny in a bathing cap. What do you do, store nuts in there?"

Gretchen put up a hand to her lumpy rubber-covered head. "It's an idea," she said, shoving away from the side. "Four more lengths, and I'll be with you."

"Regular Amazon," Dorry sputtered, but not loud enough for Gretchen to hear. She climbed out of the pool and sat waiting, wishing Gretchen would say something definite about the Nurse Corps. She'd kept her head out of the water and her make-up was still perfect. Gretchen, swimming past, said to herself again that it really was remarkable.

Preston halted the little tractor he used for cutting the grass and called across the lawn. "Doctor! Dr. Grafton."

"What'll you have, Preston?" Kenneth asked, strolling up to him.

"Just wondered how Miss Joplin is doing."

"Better. She's going home tomorrow for a few days to rest." As he spoke, Dr. Grafton rubbed a hand thoughtfully on his chin, wondering how Rosemary would make out at home.

Preston leaned both arms on the steering wheel. "She's a nice girl," he said. "The trouble is, she thinks in the past tense. Some young people do. Sensitive ones. There's time yet for her to get over it, wouldn't you say?" At Kenneth's nod he twisted around to survey the lawn. "This'll just have to do. I'm elected to hang

Japanese lanterns for the girls' dance tonight. You going to that, doctor?"

"I'm on duty."

"Too bad. Hope those two friends of yours show up. They'd give the girls a whirl. Especially Dr. Dolphin. Expect they'll be busy too?"

"Probably."

Preston, with a nod of farewell, started up the motor and roared off toward the shed. Kenneth stood watching the little red tractor for a minute, then turned toward the hospital and his room.

He'd bought a Vandebruck recording of *"Fugues from the Well-Tempered Clavichord,"* arranged by Vandebruck himself for organ. With this turned low on his phonograph, he lay down to think, and, at first, found his thoughts wandering. Eventually, like a bird following an erratic course to a definite point, they settled on Rosemary.

As she had said, it was an unusual experience to be present on the scene, so to speak, of a dream. Haltingly, then almost too fast for clarity, Rosemary had told it over and then rushed, like a stream tumbling over a rock, into recollection. "There it was, Kenneth, our life, I mean . . . going along in the most unimportant, warm way, with my father watching us both in a sort of sober happiness, and mother . . . laughing. That's all I think I remember. She'd look up from a chair when I came in from school and say, "Hallo, and how's my Rosemarie," with that pretty laugh, or come in the nights when I couldn't sleep and push nothing at me as if it were a bundle and say, "Here, one pound of sleep, only don't make a noise eating it." And then all of a sudden—nothing at all. I can't tell you what it was like—utterly empty. I could wait forever for the figure in the chair, the voice in the night, but it wouldn't be long enough. And then *she* came." Her voice leaned on the sentence and collapsed. Kenneth waited, thinking that by this rush of words she was giving herself a sort of shock therapy. She rushed on. "My stepmother is . . . her feet hurt. I know it doesn't have anything to do with anything. It always seemed to . . . she seemed to be so *pained*, between me and her feet. It was so dreadfully different. I guess I probably bothered her more than her feet, but I always thought it was the feet and it was all awfully strained and— sad—different. Provident and unlovely. And I suppose it wasn't really her fault. I know she tried . . . I mean I know it now. . . ."

Kenneth waited still, because he was young and far from sure what he actually should do. Whatever I can, he thought, I'll do. But a psychiatrist would know now whether to speak or simply remain a presence. And the part of his mind that concerned itself with himself, that ever alert part of every mind, told him that this science of psychiatry had become intrinsic with him. It would be psychiatry, and here was his first patient, arrived too early. He waited, watchfully, knowing how much she'd have to help herself. It comes to that always, after the sympathy and the understanding, you must help yourself. He tried to tell her so with his eyes. And was rewarded, in a little while, by an expression of thoughtfulness slowly replacing the daze on her face.

He risked a few words then. "Rosemary, do you always go back to the past in your dreams?"

"I think perhaps I have," she said slowly.

Have? Kenneth wondered. "And do you *think* back too?"

After a little while, she said, "Yes. That too."

"You said that, in the dream, your mother said 'forgive me.'"

Rosemary looked at him, a very level glance, not sliding her eyes obliquely away as she usually did. "I must have figured that out myself—that I've actually not forgiven her," she said in the same slow voice.

"Yes. You did."

"Oh." Briefly, she closed her eyes. When she opened them, he detected again that look of—considering. "I'm going home tomorrow, or I guess you already know," she said.

"That's good," he answered, hoping it would be.

She agreed simply, as though to reassure him. "I think so." Her lids lowered heavily again. "Must be the pill," she murmured, and fell asleep.

Now, slung across his bed, Kenneth thought of Preston. "She thinks in the past tense," he'd said. Well possibly—no, *probably*—we can put that in the past tense, Kenneth decided with a touch of pride. After all, she was his first patient and responding nicely. She'll do all right at home, he told himself. Partly on her own mettle, and partly because Mrs. Joplin is an honorable woman who will never take advantage of so diffident an emotion as change of heart.

Nelle walked briskly toward the Nurses Station, keeping her shoulders well back because Gretchen in her exasperatingly helpful way had mentioned that no single thing did as much for a girl's looks as good posture. There was no point in getting annoyed with Gretchen, who simply refused to be offended, certainly no point in ignoring her advice, which was always so darned good. Nelle with her shoulders back was a great improvement over Nelle with the studious slouch. She looked, as Mrs. Gibson remarked, like a girl with a lipstick in her pocket instead of a notebook.

"Mrs. Peder?" said the new Nelle. "Old 'Me-and-my-Brassie' in 460 says he won't have a fracture board on his bed."

Mrs. Peder locked the drug closet, turned with a puzzled expression. "Who? Oh. . . ." She laughed a little. "Mr. Chalmers. Goodness, what does he talk about since Mr. Rose left?"

154

"Nothing. The new man's a bridge fiend. They just sort of stare at each other."

"What do you mean," said Mrs. Peder, getting back to business, "he won't have the fracture board on his bed?"

"That's what he says."

"But Dr. Alvord ordered it."

"I told him. He says tell Dr. Alvord he won't have it and that's that."

Mrs. Peder closed her eyes. "Some of these men can be so cantankerous. Well, go back and tell him we called Dr. Alvord, and Dr. Alvord says does Mr. Chalmers wish to diagnose and treat himself in the future, or does he wish to retain Dr. Alvord in the capacity of physician."

Nelle laughed. "It sounds just like him."

"Oh, that's what Alvord always says if his patients start acting up. Scares them silly, and we never have a bit of trouble after that. There's no point in actually calling. It would aggravate him, and we'd get the same answer anyway. Wait a minute. . . . I'll get Harold to bring up a board and he can go in with you. Get it all over at once."

When Mr. Chalmers, utterly subdued, was installed on his fracture board, Nelle returned to Mrs. Peder.

"He took it like a man," she reported. "His putter fell out of bed."

"His *putter?*"

Nelle nodded seriously. "His son smuggled it in for him. He's been practicing one-arm putting."

"In case, I suppose, he ever has to putt lying down and can only use one arm."

"Best to be prepared," Nelle said and burst into laughter. Lately she laughed so easily, so much. Oh, it was a lovely world, with a bright summer streaming ahead, graduation coming, and

155

tonight, after work, a dance with Wally.

"How's Rosemary Joplin?" Mrs. Peder was asking.

"Rosemary? Fine. She really seems. . . . I think this illness has done her good."

"How do you mean?"

"I went up there, just before I came on. And she seemed so much happier. Miss Harker said Dr. Grafton had just been there and seemed to buck her up a lot."

"He's the medical intern, isn't he? I've heard he has that effect on lots of patients."

"Well, he sure did on Rosemary. She. . . ." But she decided against whatever revelation she'd been about to make. After all, Mrs. Peder knew very little of Rosemary's private life, and presumably didn't care much. Furthermore, it was time for dinner. "May I go down now, to eat?"

"Run along," Mrs. Peder yawned. "Goodness, I could sleep for a year. Maybe it's just the rest that's helping Miss Joplin."

"Maybe," said Nelle. But she didn't think so.

She went off for dinner, her mind popping gay as a grasshopper from Rosemary back to Wally. Or, perhaps, to her dress. Laid out on the bed in her room was an evening dress, lemon linen with brown piping on the bodice, around the hem, and the thinnest of brown shoulder straps. A pair of lemon-linen high-heeled sandals were resting neatly side by side on the floor, and on the dresser, next to her mother's perfume, was a thin gold chain with a tiny perfect emerald hanging pendant. Her mother's, too. She could see the clothes, the perfume, the little green jewel . . . waiting for her, just as she had laid them out. As soon as she got off, she would whisk back to the Residence, into the shower, (thank heaven her hair was naturally curly.) And there would be, she was sure there would be, flowers. And she hoped in a box of that cellophany stuff you could see through.

Because Wally had asked about the color of her dress and there couldn't be any other reason. So, shower, dress, flowers. . . . She said the pretty program over, bouncing into the elevator.

"Well, for a girl who deals in the sad fundamentals of life, you look rather high-spirited," dripped a disapproving voice beside her.

"Oh, do I?" Nelle said lamely to Mrs. Mew, whom she hadn't seen in ages, nor missed. She tried to look directly in Mrs. Mew's eyes, or at least at the face, but her eyes skipped away. It had always been something of a trial to regard this countenance at close range. You, she told Mrs. Mew silently, deal in the real fundamentals, and very nice ones, of life, but you always seem to be on your way to a mass burial. Aloud, she could think of nothing but oh, do I?

"You do," Mrs. Mew, darkly. "It isn't seemly at all. This is a hospital, not a . . . a gymnasium."

After all, Nelle argued with herself, I am somewhat beyond the scope of Mrs. Mew's displeasure. "I don't know," she said politely, "I rather think the psychological effect of a good temper is better than. . . . Is better."

"Psychology," Mrs. Mew snorted. "You girls are filled with that nonsense." She got off the elevator and paced angrily beside the girl. "In my day we didn't think of that. We thought of healing."

"I believe they now go hand in hand," Nelle observed demurely.

Mrs. Mew lined up behind her at the cafeteria counter, shoving her tray along relentlessly close. Nelle was stricken with a sudden fear that she actually planned for them to sit together. For what possible reason, she couldn't think, but it must, at all costs, be avoided. She wanted to think beautiful things for a full half-hour, and a beautiful thought in the company of Mrs. Mew could be likened to a butterfly in January. It *might* happen, but Nelle wouldn't wish to stay put till it did. Her eyes roved frantically over the room, roosted like a pair of fluttered birds on a table with one remaining seat. She sped for it, not glancing back till she was seated. Mrs. Mew stood several feet away, her harsh face rather wiped of expression as she turned her head from side to side looking for a place to sit. She turned and moved slowly in the other direction.

"Oh, my gosh," Nelle said plaintively.

"What's the gripe?" one of the students inquired without much interest.

"Nothing, I guess." She picked up knife and fork, held them motionless over her plate. It just wasn't fair. People who go around making everybody miserable with their bad dispositions shouldn't make them more so by being suddenly pathetic. It simply wasn't *fair*. Well, she wasn't going to let it bother her. So Mrs. Mew was lonely. So what? If she had the brains of a mosquito, she'd figure out why. But it took, she thought, picking up the salt, it took some of the seasoning out of things. She returned to the contemplation of shower, dress, flowers, with a little effort at first, then with almost unimpaired relish.

At the other end of the dining room, Mrs. Mew chewed steadily and wondered why everything inside her felt so stony. These students, she said to herself with an attempt at indignation. Their mincing, their airs! But her outrage felt flat. I suppose, she wondered on, that it's the last time I'll see that one too. None of them ever says good-by to me, not unless they happen to see me in the hall as they tear off from graduation. The wretched, mean, ungrateful. . . . She broke off the silent words, because her hand was beginning to tremble, because she was afraid of accidentally speaking aloud. Dully her glance moved around the room from the empty table at which she sat. The

158

nurse who had been there had hastily finished her coffee, departed with a nod. Oh, they run away quickly enough, she assured herself, when they see someone whose sense of duty rebukes them. This reasoning offered scant comfort. The fretful eyes sharpened. There, over at that table, when the student on the inside leaned down, there was definitely the outline of a pack of cigarettes in the pocket beneath her bib. Smoking, are you? thought Mrs. Mew. Well, we'll just see about that, Miss Flibbertigibbet, we'll just very well see about that.

Crisply uniformed, Gretchen in the garden moved toward a window of the Residence Reception Room. She was on her way to Pediatrics, but a moment stolen for a glimpse of the Japanese lanterns representing one of her dollars (representing, she corrected, one of her dollars three times in the past two years) was permissible. What she would have liked, of course, was to see Wally and Nelle, but since Nelle would only be getting off now she'd have to be content with the lanterns and the surprisingly full room of people. It looked colorful and whirling, as a dance should, and the mended lanterns with their soft lights were not a bit tawdry. Dorry hadn't done badly.

Hands on hips, she leaned forward a little at the window. To doctors Horner and Dolphin, ambling over to look too, she presented a very elegant figure. It was Dr. Dolphin who had once referred to her as "Bemis de Milo," but his interest, if it could even be called that, was in her beauty alone. Dr. Dolphin was quite sincere about his search for the pot of gold. In her way, though, he found Gretchen quite entrancing. He decided now that she looked more like a Valkyrie than a statue of Venus. She had that Nordic splendor.

"Evening, Brunhilda," he said at her side. "Dance with me?"

159

Gretchen turned her head slightly, glanced sideways at him, then down at her blue and white clothes. "Sorry, doctor, I'm not dressed for dancing."

"Forget your horse, Brunhilda?" Dr. Dolphin, as can be seen, enjoyed his own whimsy.

"Nope," said Gretchen, straightening and regarding him with large eyes. "My shield."

"You made a good decision," said Dr. Horner. "He may look like he'd be pretty smooth, Miss Bemis, but he dances like something in an obstacle race."

This was outrageously untrue, but Dolph could only scowl, since Miss Bemis with a smile for both had taken herself off. "Nice girl," Dr. Horner approved. Dr. Dolphin shrugged. "Come on," he said. "We're due back. This appears a sedate enough brawl."

"Well, of course," Horner said meekly, "It isn't the Debutante Cotillion, but we call it home."

"I hope I don't, for long."

"Well, who knows, you may yet ride to the office in your wife's Rolls Royce."

"And what would be wrong with that? Don't tell me you're one of these mutts who thinks the forty-thousand-a-year men are all fakes?"

"Oh, rubbish. I just don't think you should figure to get there on a connubial stepping stone. Not figure it, mind you. If it happens, that's gravy."

"That's just where you're wrong, my boy. A man gets what he goes after."

Dr. Horner waved his hands. "It's impossible to argue with you. You're a type. Can't get along without types."

"Surest thing you know. Now take Grafton. He's a type too. Lord, how he'd love to get a diagnosis and then have to de-

160

fend it courageously against the combined scorn of all the bigwigs. He'd be right in the end, naturally, or he wouldn't be a type. Oh, I wanna be a doctor like. . . ."

"Oh, shut up," Horner interrupted. "Grafton's okay. He's a type like the rest of us except you, just doing his best to be a good doctor, and he's not trying to locate Easy Street through a stethescope. I think he's right, you go to too many movies."

"Oh well, don't get huffy," Dolph said, somewhat discomfited. It confused him that when he was doing his best to sound sophisticated was just when Ken or Horner chose to needle him. Dr. Dolphin's ego maintained a tenuous balance between his own brashness and the opinions of others. The more he valued the latter, the less he controlled the former, and he fluctuated constantly between conceit and deflation.

"Huffy?" Dr. Horner said. "Why should I get huffy? It's your own character you're ruining, not mine."

"Oh, well," Dolph said again. Their white figures blurred and disappeared in the darkness of the lawn as they walked back to the hospital.

And the funny part is, Dr. Horner said to himself as he entered Emergency and blinked at the tiled glare, the funny part is, Dolph's a good doctor.

"It's a crazy business," he mumbled.

"You're telling me," said a student at the desk. But she only said it to be agreeable. There hadn't been a thing to do since dinner and now she was off for two days and so far as she was concerned things were just dandy.

"Night, doctor," she said gaily and flipped off. Those interns, gripe, gripe, gripe, she thought, and then forgot in the sudden decision to get dressed and run down to the dance. She didn't have a date, but you can never tell what will happen.

When she got to the shower room, Nelle Gibson was already in a streaming stall, bathing cap anchored firmly beneath her chin, enough lather to do a Monday wash, her voice raised high in song.

"*Come then, maidens and men to the da-de-dum-dum-dum. . .*" she caroled over the splashing water. And then, "Oh, hi Murphy," as she stepped out of the stall.

"Hi. You going to this dance?"

"I surely am. You?"

"No," said Murphy, reversing herself. She wasn't too sorry. "It's better to go to bed than to a dance without the proper accessories," she explained.

"Oh? Anything I can lend you? Not that I haven't borrowed everything but my dress from Mother," Nelle offered, pulling on a robe.

"The sort of accessory I meant was a man."

"Gosh, Murphy. . . ."

"I didn't mean anything. I could have got a date, only I didn't think till a few minutes ago that I'd be interested. It sounds like fun, though. You'd better hurry."

Nelle ripped the cap off and ran down the hall. Fifteen minutes later, she stood before the mirror in the beautiful gown, a cluster of tiny green orchids pinned over her excited heart, a drift of her Mother's perfume on the hem of her skirt, the orchids and emerald calling forth an elusive auburn in the brown of her brushed curls. Never before, perhaps never again in quite this way, was Nelle's mirrored image such an ornamental pleasure. Behind her, on the bed, lay the open transparent box in which she'd found Wally's flowers. Before her, on the bureau, was his card, with the slanting script, "*For the Gibson Girl.*" And, she looked at her clock, and just one hour of dancing. . . .

From her room in the Infirmary atop the Residence, Rosemary could hear the faraway strains of music, the silly, pretty little dance tunes. She listened vaguely, stretching with a charmed slow balance, still tired though she'd slept more than waked today. Of all the days in many years she could remember, this had been the most important. Importance, she thought, is very fatiguing. She lay there, imagining herself to be like a shell, a bottle perhaps, that has been emptied and now, quite clear, awaits refilling.

In the night, the church bells sounded. Near by, the measured deep swinging of the bells in the Catholic steeple. Behind them, a little later, a little higher, like the call of a bittern, the voice of the Presbyterian bells. And very far away, merging like an echo, the darkling midnight bells of her father's church.

Chapter 14.

SPRING, idling along, barefoot goosegirl in a meadow, suddenly gathered up her skirts and fled into the arms of summer.

On the sun roof, the patients talked to each other about themselves. In beds, wheelchairs and on foot, they'd come to sit, back a little out of the sunshine, and smell the flowery air. And to talk. . . .

"I tell you, there's no such thing as spot reducing. Either you take it all off or depend on a girdle. . ."

"You did? Well, just let me tell you about mine. . . ."

"And so they sent Aunty to Arizona to die. That was thirty years ago and she's been making a mint ever since, raising alfalfa or something. . . ."

"Of course I'm tired of lying down. What I say is, you can't live by bed alone. . . ."

In the operating room, the graduate who longed for something exciting to do selected a knife from the shining Mayo tray, slapped it in the waiting palm of Dr. Alvord. The knife hung motionless a moment, descended in a swift sure arc.

With a lean cry the ambulance drew to a halt, attendants slid the stretcher out and moved with smooth haste through the door of Emergency. Dr. Horner strode, watchfully attentive, beside the blanketed figure of a man who hadn't seen the truck parked on the other side of the hill.

In Pediatrics, a small girl leaned through the bars of her bed, offered a slim red box to the boy in the next bed. "Have a piece of candy?" she invited.

The boy looked at the box, at the lender. "There's nothing in it."

"I know. It's pretend candy."

"Oh." He took a pretend piece, chewed thoughtfully. "Good. What kind is it?"

"Rosemarie de Paris."

"What's Paree?"

"It's a kind of chocolate. My father buys it for my mother. She ate this. Ate it first, I mean." Her lips began to tremble. "I want to go home. . . ."

"Why?" asked her friend with cool curiosity.

"Because my mother's there. . . ." The tears splashed rapidly.

"Oh. Well, so's mine, but I don't want to."

"Nurse!" wailed the little girl. "Nurse!"

"Miss Joplin, prepare an ether bed, please. Immediately. Patient coming up from Emergency."

"Yes, Mrs. Peder," said Rosemary, already on her way to the linen room. She swept the sheets tight, folded them back sideways the length of the bed, went quickly to the Utility Room for hot-water bottles. She said a little prayer, but now for the first time the prayer was offered truly for the patient, and not for a frightened Rosemary.

Gretchen was in her room, packing in a desultory fashion

that involved putting blouses she'd thought were still in Ohio back in the closet because after she'd gotten them out there appeared to be no more room on the bed. Therefore she'd probably do better to clear up the bed, only half the stuff there could easily be thrown out if she had a box to throw it in, so on the whole a trip to the kitchen to locate a box would be wisest, except that on the way there she glanced into Nelle's room, found Nelle in occupancy, and so abandoned her packing.

"What are you doing?" she asked, pausing in the doorway.

"Well, for heaven's sake, *look*," said Nelle, throwing an arm around to indicate a confusion of dresses, uniforms, shoes, books and the ill-conceived oil by Aunt May scattered over bed, floor, and bureau.

"Me too, only I had to stop for a box."

"Get me one too, will you?"

"I'm not going. I decided to talk to you instead."

Nelle looked around, shoved a heap of stuff off a chair, pushed another pile to the head of the bed and sank with a sigh. "All right. Let's talk."

"You name a subject."

"Can't. I'm a subject myself."

Gretchen deliberated. She could think of little to say, or perhaps too much. She remembered how in high school the last weeks before graduation had inched along, with everyone crying for it to come, wouldn't it ever *come*. And then, so suddenly, the weeks sped away and there it was, Graduation Day, with shining sun and white gowns, corsages, and weeping mothers, and in themselves a fluttering reluctance. How she'd looked with envy on the safe and carefree juniors. They had still the whole lovely senior year before them. The privileges, the security. Her eyes had looked with solemn newness at the school, with its random board, worn grey floors, and large old rooms. Graduation Day. She'd longed for it, planned for it, sworn it would never come. But it had, and she'd gone into miserable privacy and wept the night before. And there'd been a boy . . . Colin. She didn't even know where Colin was now. He'd been brushed and blond, and she remembered his laugh. Colin had had an athletic letter sewed on his white wool sweater, but he wore the sweater inside out, so the letter was obvious, but it looked as if Colin didn't care. She remembered that, and his laughter, and the night they sat in his car, holding hands, kissing just now and then, but mostly sitting in silence and sadness because he was going away and they were in love. Gretchen, then a passionate reader of Swinburne, had turned to him and said, "Colin, I know you don't like poetry much . . . but let me tell you a bit of one?"

Colin, surprised, assented.

"This," said Gretchen,

> "I remember the day we parted,
> The day and the way we met.
> We hoped we were both broken hearted
> And knew we should both forget."

Colin hadn't liked it much, but he'd given a reluctant smile, and in a little while they'd driven home. Now she didn't even know where he was.

Of course, that was a long time ago, and training wasn't high school. But the feeling was there, the wish to fly to the safety of last year. She'd never have a room again with red curtains and green swags. . . .

"Funny," she said, "How you can know you don't want something, but miss it just the same."

Nelle lifted her head cautiously. Did that mean. . . .Was she talking about Wally?

"I was thinking about my curtains," Gretchen went on. If she knew what Nelle was thinking, there was no indication in her tone. "Red curtains and green swags are really in awful taste."

"I've always liked them."

"So have I," Gretchen sighed. "So have I."

Nelle picked up a starched flaring student cap, turned it slowly around, balanced on a fingertip, spinning it with the other hand. "We won't be wearing them much longer."

In silence they thought of the tiny organdy graduate caps soon to be placed where the training caps had perched so proudly.

†"My mother says they look like organdy cupcakes," Nelle said pensively.

"The graduate caps?" Gretchen smiled. "You know, they do rather."

The little fluted cups, the badge, the prize. You'd done a job and done it well, for see, this little nonsense is on your head to prove it.

They sighed again.

"Do you feel sad?" Gretchen asked.

"Sort of, I guess. It's always sad to say good-by."

It isn't easy, Gretchen thought. To say good-by to a room, to part of your life. To a person. It will be like Colin, she told herself. We'll just forget. Or, of course, Dr. Whitney won't even remember to forget. I'll forget, though. Oh, naturally. And the ache within that had nothing to do with a room or green curtains grew and grew.

"Did you see that notice about the Army?" Nelle asked.

"Who hasn't?" Gretchen turned her head a little. "Are you going to apply?"

"No."

"You'd go further than the Kentucky mountains that way, I imagine," Gretchen said teasingly, wondering why in the world Nelle wanted to pretend, in their conversations, that no such person as Wally existed. She wouldn't even mention his name. "Oh well, I don't suppose I would either. Not unless they really needed nurses badly."

"Don't they?"

"No. They're taking volunteers, but Miss Merkle says they're getting enough. The Reserve's more important, I guess, but I'm going to wait about that too. I'd sort of like to do nursing that has something to do with children."

"That's easy."

"Not Pediatrics. Not in the hospital, anyway. I don't know. It'll work out."

Nelle began to make tentative swipes at her packing. "I think you're right about Rosemary, about not being in love with Grafton, I mean."

"I hope not."

"Why?"

"*Cured yesterday of my disease, I died last night of my physician,*" Gretchen quoted.

"Now what does that mean?"

"I just think it would be better if she'd . . . changed, which she has . . . for herself, and not for love of someone else."

Nelle opened a drawer with an impatient tug. "What difference does it make what causes a change, so long as it happens?"

"Because, sometimes the change won't last unless the cause does "

"You're awfully cynical about it."

"I don't think so. And I do think it's wonderful how much—steadier she is in the last couple of weeks." Nelle seemed to have stopped listening, so Gretchen fell silent, thinking about last night when Rosemary had come practically dancing in to talk. . . .

Rosemary had come to Gretchen's room the night before for no particular reason except to demonstrate her own new confidence, like a bauble. Gretchen had always awed Rosemary a bit, in spite of her friendliness, her generosity that sometimes wasn't welcome. Gretchen was so aggravatingly sure of herself, and not making a point of it was even worse.

Gretchen had been lying on her bed, in white stockings and slip. Her shoes and uniform were out, ready to be put on when she went on duty in about two hours.

"Hi, Gretchen," Rosemary greeted, sticking her head in the door.

Gretchen sat up, got up. "Come on in. Here, let me get this stuff off the chair and you can sit down."

"What are you going to do after graduation?" Rosemary asked as soon as she sat. "Have you decided?"

"Believe it or not, no. I'm going back home and think about it." Gretchen frowned with sudden concentration, then looked up with a delighted smile. "Say, why don't you come home with me, for part of the summer? Mother would *love* it. We could really have a wonderful time at the lake."

"Oh gosh, Gretchen," Rosemary breathed. She seemed to be fairly bursting with words put aside, and breathless with the ones substituted. "I'd have to think. I mean, I have a plan and I can't say anything about it yet, till it works, if it does. But I'd just adore going out there. Do you . . . would it be all right if I came a little later, say a couple of weeks after you go?"

"Well, sure. We'll take you any time."

"That'd be so nice," Rosemary said, leaning back in the yellow chair.

But on the whole, Gretchen decided now, it probably would be a good idea to say nothing about it to Nelle yet. Until Rosemary's plan, whatever it was, worked out.

"Mother is so excited about the graduation ceremony," Nelle was saying. "She's wild about the idea of our carrying candles."

"It's symbolic in more ways than one."

"How's that?"

"Oh, sometimes we remind me of a lot of moths, fluttering at candles and hoping they won't burn. Yes, that's what we are, moths," she decided, getting up to leave.

"Well," said Nelle, "we'll either get burned by candles or hit by swatters, I suppose."

Gretchen, as usual, had the last word. "It's a wise moth that knows its own swatter," she said at the door, and feeling she couldn't improve on that went to the kitchen for a box.

The room looked more of a mess than ever now. She scowled at the litter of clothes and possessions, dumped a few things in the throwing-out box, changed her mind and retrieved a couple, and ultimately sighed with despair. I'll have to call in a moving company, she decided gloomily, and sat down on a heap of dresses. The Hobo Clown mused in his frame with unaltered wit and pensiveness. She wouldn't take him down till the last.

Oh well, she decided, getting up, I guess I'll go down for lunch. Nelle, when asked, said she had already eaten and did Gretchen know it was hot dogs and sauerkraut today.

"That does it," Gretchen fumed. Riding down in the elevator, she decided to buy lunch at the Coffee Shop.

Dr. Bradley was at the counter, drinking a chocolate malted, eating cookies.

"Hello, doctor," Gretchen said, climbing on a stool beside her.

"Oh, Miss Bemis, I'm glad to see you. In fact, I was going to look you up this afternoon."

"You were?" Gretchen asked, pleased. "Egg salad on toast and a coffee frosted, okay Bitsy?"

"Yes," the doctor went on. "I had an idea. That is, if you're still undecided about your future."

"I'd certainly like to hear what you think."

"Why don't you go into Public Health nursing? Had you thought of it?"

"Oh, I have," Gretchen said. "That is, I've thought of Public

Health, not exactly for myself, but just generally, because I admire the program."

"I've thought, from the questions you've asked in class, that you were interested in preventive medicine. You've had two years of college, haven't you?"

Gretchen nodded.

"That's fine. Of course, you'd need more training, but not too much. The main thing is, you'd be where you would fit best."

"You know," Gretchen said slowly, "I have a feeling I've been heading in the general direction of Public Health, even if I didn't know it myself. Not," she added hastily, "that I don't appreciate...."

Dr. Bradley interrupted, "I understand." She finished her drink, prepared to rush off again. "I'd be interested to know what you decide. Let me hear from you, won't you?"

"I certainly will. And, Dr. Bradley, thank you very much. You've been ... very kind to me, all along."

"I've been glad to be. Good-by, and whatever you do, good luck." And in her customary manner, Dr. Bradley disappeared like a salamander up a chimney.

"Miss Bemis?"

Gretchen looked up from her sandwich. "Mmm, Bitsy?"

"I just thought ... in case you don't get back here before you graduate, that I'd like to say what the doctor said. Good-by and good luck, you know."

"That's nice, Bitsy." Gretchen studied the pert face with its unusually sober expression. "But I'll probably be in often before that."

"Well, just in case," Bitsy repeated doggedly.

"Then, the same to you, and thanks," Gretchen said, a little surprised at this demonstration of friendliness from Bitsy, who customarily reserved her smiles and the best pie for interns, but pleased nevertheless.

Presently she returned to her packing in better spirits and accomplished most of it without trouble. The room looked strange now. Not hers any more. In the closet a few uniforms, a couple of dresses hung, with empty hangers strung along the pole. The curtains, the bedspread, the pictures from her bureau, all packed to go home by Express. She planned to carry Emmett Kelly with her on the train.

She lay down on the bed and thought . . . about Rosemary, graduation, the emptying rooms. About Public Health, and her mother's coming in a couple of days, and Prudence. She thought about Dr. Whitney, and rolled over to bury her face in the pillow. Because he'd never said another word about seeing her again, and the ache in her heart that had nothing to do with emptying rooms or Prudence or Public Health just grew and grew. There was no way to stop it.

Chapter 15.

MRS. GIBSON'S dinner party occurred not the day after graduation, but the Saturday before. She'd found to her astonishment she could gather all the necessary people on that night—always a difficulty with so unpredictable a lot as the medical. With that settled, everything else, such as the probable departure of Gretchen and Mrs. Bemis right after graduation, fell into line. Everything, thought Mrs. Gibson, who had never read Voltaire, happens for the best.

At five o'clock on Saturday afternoon, she sat at her dressing table, patting her beautiful bluish hair, running a bright selecting eye over her perfumes. Not *Tzigane*, she thought. Marvelous with dark colors but somehow uncomfortable with pastels. And anyway, she searched again, anyway, it didn't seem to be here. Oh, yes. She'd given it to Nelle. Well. . . .

Afternoon sunlight fanned through the blinds. Mellow and unsubstantial, it lay about the lavender and purple bedroom. "Eva!" May had shrieked when informed of redecoration plans, "Eva—you aren't going to put *Archer* in a purple bedroom!" Archer had red hair and a red face. "Oh, yes," Mrs. Gibson had said, pleased for once to be on the shocking end of things with May, "Oh, certainly." Archer's red top was definitely a *touch*.

Whirlwind, she decided, and touched her ear lobes, the hem of her skirt.

She hummed happily going downstairs. Everything was just so lovely. Archer was home and had apparently sold acres of oilcloth. Ugly stuff, she thought affectionately. The house was simply ashimmer with cleanliness and new summer covers. So wise, all that yellow in the living room, with its Wedgewood blue walls. Last year's motif, purple and green, had looked divine in *Town and Country*, but rather like blotting paper when you got it home and paid for.

Archer, waiting in the center hall, received a sweet smile from his descending wife. It was just as well he didn't know the smile attached less to him than to two sets of covers and drapes in as many years.

"You look mighty happy," he said approvingly.

Mrs. Gibson tipped back her head to look into her husband's broad red face. "Oh, I am. It's wonderful to have you home." She slipped a hand into his arm. "I do adore yellow."

Archer considered this. "Why don't you get one?"

"One what?"

"Yellow dress. Isn't that what you meant?"

"Oh now, really, darling. A yellow dress. What can you be thinking of?" She released him gently, after an appraising glance at the living room, hummed off to the kitchen.

Archer, accustomed to being left in mild confusion, looked through the living room for an inspection of his own. Very pretty, but with a plumped-up waiting appearance which automatically forbid entry, much less the reading of an evening paper. Well, there was still ample light on the terrace. It's good to be home, he thought. Archer was a rare man. He enjoyed his wife's dinner parties.

Corinna Svenson, Mrs. Gibson's cook, maid, general advisor, liked dinner parties too. This one, she thought, for Nelle and her friends, would be extra good. Because it seemed that at last the bookworm showed signs of becoming a butterfly. And that, thought Corinna, may not be good biology for insects, but it's excellent for girls.

"Coming along fine, Mrs. Gibson," she said, casting a proud eye around the kitchen, sniffing with delicate complacence at the fragrant food, prepared solely by her hand. For Mrs. Gibson had sound ideas about cooks, never offering to help with sauces, rustle up pies—generally glad to leave the menu to Corinna's discretion. On the stove, a great glazed ham, decorated with pineapple and candied cherries awaited a final trip to the oven. Several pans of yeast rolls were rising steadily to their consummation. Little shiny lima beans, representing several hours of shelling on the part of Mrs. Gibson, who enjoyed few things more than to sit in her sunny velvet-beed garden and prepare vegetables, were washed for cooking. A large wooden bowl, dishtowel-covered, held the salad—watercress, endive, tomatoes. In the ice box, spiced cantaloupe and olives were chilling in cut glass, side by side with the grapefruit and almond sherbet.

"It looks heavenly," Mrs. Gibson sighed.

"Should be tasty enough," Corinna agreed, oiling the scrubbed skins of Idaho potatoes and slipping them in the oven.

Mrs. Gibson, who was beginning to prickle a little, wondered how in the world Corinna, really quite heavy, could not mind the heat of the kitchen, ventilator or no. But there she was, in a green cotton dress, crisp and cool as one of her own pickles.

"Aren't you hot?" Mrs. Gibson asked helplessly. "I mean, it seems we could have planned something a little less. . . ."

"Can't cook a meal without using the oven," Corinna interrupted. "I don't hold one bit with these cold meals in summer. If you want a picnic, then you should go into the woods for one. But you can't feed a picnic to folks in a dining room. You'd better go out of here before your hair starts down."

"Perhaps I should. Has Mr. Hartwig come yet?"

"Didn't you hear him?" Corinna laughed nervously. "He's in the dining room, setting the table." She lifted a hand for silence. "I have never known a man so quiet. Maybe," she went on in a lowered tone, "when you go in to check on the table, you could, uh, compliment him on his new uniform. He borrowed it especially for this occasion. I must say, it surely is good of you to have him buttle this way. He liked it lots last time. I *think* he'll do better at the serving tonight, having read a book on it recently. . . ." For Corinna, the words were strangely hectic, too fast, as though she spoke to conceal.

"That's thoughtful of him," Mrs. Gibson said. "I . . . suppose it wouldn't hurt." She recalled the first time Mr. Hartwig had been pressed into service when she'd had so many (sixteen, wasn't it?) for dinner that Corinna, unequal to both cooking and serving, had produced this, her uncle, as "butler." He was a retired seaman, who lived in a seaman's home. The Club, he called it. He'd been delighted to come out and help his niece.

"Not that I'm saying anything against the Club, you know," he'd told Mrs. Gibson when they met. "It's fine there. Very clean. The beds are tin, but they're painted brown to represent something or other, and look very good. And the vacuum cleaner comes in once a week. But you know how it is. A man gets tired of doing nothing." His bright brown eyes roved favorably about the kitchen.

"Have you . . . ever done any waiting on table?" Mrs. Gibson had asked, already so charmed by him that the question was purposeless.

"Not one bit," he answered heartily, whisking his fist before him. "Can't see there'd be any difficulty. Just a case of getting the dishes on when they're loaded and off when they're empty. eh?"

"Well . . ." said Mrs. Gibson in the tone of a woman unable to resist buying something she doesn't need and knows she can't use. "Well, there's a little more to it. . . ."

"I think Uncle will manage," Corinna said in the tone of a woman who's just bought something elaborate that she isn't sure will work.

Two willing but dubious women looked at each other, while Mr. Hartwig resumed his inspection of the kitchen. With a white jacket over his blue-serge pants, Corinna's uncle had served the meal. In one respect, he was superb. He moved with the nearest approach to soundlessness that Mrs. Gibson had ever known. You'd hardly know he was here, she thought, and looked up to discover he wasn't. Because Mr. Hartwig, propelled on his quiet feet by an innocent love of gracious homes, kept disappearing between courses into the living room, the hall, the terrace. He served and removed impartially from right or left, and Mrs. Gibson realized with despair that neither she nor Corinna had told him not to stack the plates as he took them away. Well, it's too late to do anything now, she thought, smiling pleasantly into the startled and amused faces at her table, lifting her shoulders ever so faintly at her husband's brows lifting from the other end of it.

Now, at Corinna's assurance that he'd read a book (Mrs. Post?) she relaxed. Because she hated to say anything at all to Mr. Hartwig that wasn't friendly and approving. "He has that effect on everybody," Corinna had said. "Even me."

"Well," said Mrs. Gibson, "I'll just go in and see how he's making out."

Corinna looked after her doubtfully. She was rather fond of her employer, fonder of her employer's daughter. Mrs. Gibson would have been amazed, but amused, to know that Corinna's regard for both of them was based, in good part, on pity. There they were, she would think, round peg and square hole, hopefully trying to fit. Except, Corinna corrected now, the square peg showed definite signs of deserting the unequal effort.

Corinna stretched and reverted to a former thought. If Nelle was a bookworm about to become a butterfly, then her mother was the snuggest of unhatchable cocoons, wrapped round in lace and linen and as little likely to emerge as a fly from amber.

In her accustomed happy state of unawareness, Mrs. Gibson skimmed into the dining room. The door swung to and slapped her, but she, intent on staring at Mr. Hartwig, paid no heed. Mr. Hartwig, intent on studying the table, did not heed her entry.

Here in the quiet dining room, diffused late sunshine slanted across the table. Grey linen, yellow snapdragons, old polished silver and goblets that really glittered. They were using the Royal Worcester and Steuben crystal. The table, Mrs. Gibson told herself nervously, looks beautiful. *Beautiful*, she repeated. But a sort of shriek rose in her mind, and she felt like sitting on the floor and crying.

"Mr. Hartwig?" she said on a piteous note. "Mr. Hartwig?"

In bottle-green coat and breeches of vermilion, Mr. Hartwig bowed. "At your pleasure," he said.

"Oh, *no!*"

Mr. Hartwig's face was wrinkled, his eyes slanted merrily, his mouth was wide with a smile.

Mrs. Gibson backed into the kitchen. "The frog footman," she mumbled. "He looks like the frog footman." She turned to Corinna, accusation on her lovely smooth face. "Did you say *compliment* him?" she inquired in a glazed voice. "What is this, a dinner or a—a fancy dress ball?"

Corinna was sad but unsurprised. "I thought you might see it that way...."

"You thought? Corinna, you *couldn't* have been thinking. What ... *thinking?*" She felt completely incoherent. She'd never believed till now that you could be stunned right out of your language. But Hartwig's—livery, his white stockings and patent leather shoes, his . . . it . . . the whole incredible ensemble drove the meaning of speech from her tongue.

Corinna watched with stiff sympathy, unable to align herself on either side.

Mrs. Gibson said without direction, "I wish I could lie down with an ice bag on my feet."

"On your feet?" Mr. Hartwig had come through the swinging door.

She nodded, eyes on the floor. "It does something soothing to the blood." Past reason now, she thought, past care.

"Do tell," said Mr. Hartwig.

Mrs. Gibson's glance traveled over the floor, rested, not without wincing, on the patent-leather pumps. They look like ballet shoes, she decided. With a sudden effort, she looked directly on the gently happy features of her once-in-a-way butler. I can't tell him to take them off, she wailed. How can I hurt such a pleased child? But the specter of her dinner table circled round by this brilliant curiosity was too much. They'll think it's a circus. I don't even *know* Mrs. Bemis or the Joplins.

She took a deep breath, straightened, spoke in what she felt was her closest approach yet to grande damishness. "*Mr. Hartwig.*" The regal note failed. "Mr. Hartwig," she said imploringly. "Where did you get . . . it?" waving her hands weakly.

"My livery? From an actor. We had a play last night given by these troupers. Lots of people come down to the Club to entertain us. I was very kindly given permission to wear these for tonight." He smoothed bottle-green tails over his boney hips. "A nice fit. And a touch of tone." He was still in no doubt as to the effect of his borrowed feathers. He took Mrs. Gibson's stammering for an extreme of admiration. Corinna, Mrs. Gibson recalled, had said her uncle wasn't outstandingly brainy. Well, it isn't easier to hurt a slow-thinking old man. It's much much harder. She looked plaintively at Corinna, who regarded her sympathetically. Apparently that was as much as Corinna intended to do, just understand. She didn't open her mouth.

"Just a minute, please," Mrs. Gibson said with sudden decision. She turned and almost ran to the terrace. "Archer? Archer! Come here, please. *Please*. . . ."

"Good heavens, Eva," her husband said, getting up from his chair, "What's the trouble?"

"Archer, come with me please. You must settle this, because I can't. If I live through this dinner, you'll have to take me away somewhere for a rest. I tell you, it's too much. . . ." She babbled back to the kitchen.

Archer, dangling his unfinished paper, followed slowly. He was used to alarums and excursions.

"What's *that?*" he shouted at the kitchen door, then licked his lips and said more composedly. "Could someone explain? Mr. Hartwig, that's you, isn't it?"

Gravely, proudly, Mr. Hartwig bowed. "At your pleasure," he said.

Mrs. Gibson decided she heard a car coming. She fled without a backward glance.

And now, dinner past, they were assembled in the living room, with coffee. Gently the odor of clematis stole through the open windows and lost itself in the lady-perfumed air. Even Mrs. Joplin had made a modest purchase of cologne for this occasion.

Mrs. Gibson was happy and at ease. Archer, of course, had managed. Mr. Hartwig, in white jacket, had served admirably. (It must certainly have been Mrs. Post.) Silent, attentive, he had gone through course after course, showing no inclination to stack or stray away. Mrs. Gibson wished his face hadn't been quite so dejected, but after all, even a darling old man like Mr. Hartwig couldn't be allowed to flout the laws of good taste.

Nervously, she brushed off recollection of his old eyes reproachful above the shrimp cocktail.

She surveyed her guests with an expert glance. Lovely, everybody talking. Not that she couldn't have whipped things to a proper state if there had been signs of remissness, but it's always so much better if they carry the ball themselves. She reviewed her company again, decided it was safe to concentrate on Gretchen's mother. Marvelously organized woman, she was. The sort who has *interests*, who never gets in a rut, decided Mrs. Gibson.

"And how is Ohio?" she asked Mrs. Bemis, who had an impulse to say, "better thanks."

"Getting along, with the help of Senator Taft," she substituted.

"Taft?" said Mrs. Gibson doubtfully. "Is he from Ohio? I thought Washington."

For a moment, Mrs. Bemis thought she was being gently joshed, but a glance at Mrs. Gibson's innocently interested face convinced her it was not so. "Well," she said slowly, "Perhaps you're thinking of someone else. . . ."

"The president, perhaps. Or his father. The one who got so enormously fat," Mrs. Gibson said without conviction.

Mrs. Bemis glanced about for help, but everyone in the room seemed occupied, except Gretchen, who was listening with a sort of fascination and refused to meet her mother's eye.

Now how, Mrs. Bemis thought, could I . . . perhaps. . . . "Mrs. Gibson," she said brightly. "Did you by any chance see the article in this morning's *Times*, the one on cortisone?" This, she decided, should answer much.

"Oh, no," Mrs. Gibson was saying regretfully. "To be truthful, I simply never do read the *Times*, or any other paper, come to that."

"Never at all?"

"No. I mean, don't you think things are bad enough without having it authoritatively outlined every morning in the *Times?* The way I look at it is, when I get up, I feel much too good to read the papers, and by evening I'm too tired."

Her suspicions justified, Mrs. Bemis dared a look at her daughter, who stared placidly over a bowl of poppies to the opposite wall.

Mrs. Gibson rose. "I must see to. . . . How very nice to have you here. Your daughter is one of my special pets, you know." She trailed off with a backward smile.

Mrs. Bemis sat back on the couch, biting her lip a little. She turned to Gretchen.

"She's very nice," Gretchen said blandly.

Her mother nodded. "Your father won't believe a word of this," she predicted. "Neither do I."

"You get used to the way Mrs. Gibson talks."

"You do?" Mrs. Bemis sounded as though she'd need better credentials than just someone's word. "Your Wally seems quite attentive to the daughter?"

"He's not my Wally. I think perhaps he's Nelle's Wally. Or will be."

"Prudence will be very annoyed. 'But *Gret,* he's so simply civilized!'" Pru's airy voice fluted convincingly from solid Mrs. Bemis.

Gretchen smiled. "I like Wally very much and would much prefer to see him with Nelle." That seemed a clear statement, so she went on, "How's Sheridan?"

"We haven't seen much of Sheridan lately," Mrs. Bemis said, in a tone suitable for observing, "We haven't seen much bad weather lately."

Mrs. Joplin, on the down-filled couch by the hearth, inspected the company with interest, careful not to let her eyes dwell too long on Rosemary. Fearful of overshooting the lengths to which their new relationship might safely take them. As though she and Rosemary had struck an unworded bargain to move slowly, and she now honored the bargain. Mrs. Joplin knew to a nicety how long Aaron would submit to being Michael the Irish fisherman, at what point to redirect Margaret's amazing creativeness, how long even the most interested children would listen to Bible stories before getting down to baseball. She could balance housekeeping, parish problems, and the delicate task of inflating Dr. Joplin's constantly ebbing ego. Her efforts had been useless with Rosemary. From the first blunder, when she'd asked if Rosemary would like to call her Mother, all useless. And now, after it seemed no longer to matter, was she to find a footing on the sands of her relationship with Rosemary? And sand, she thought now, is—was—a good word for it. Between us we created a desert. She sighed, not at all sure yet whether the relief that seemed burgeoning was oasis or mirage. She sighed because it did still matter, very much.

"More coffee?"

She turned to Mrs. Gibson, followed by the disconsolate butler with a tray.

"No, thank you. That was a magnificent dinner," Mrs. Joplin said with the measured respect of one good cook approving another.

"Oh, I'm so glad you liked it, I know Corinna's pleased and that's so important. Aren't you in a simple *fantod* over the graduation?" Mrs. Gibson plumped down beside her. "Isn't it nice that we meet at *last*, though of course I've been listening to your bells for years—they don't sound quite so *doomish* as the others, if you know what I mean. Rosemary looks a perfect dream tonight, like a fairy in a pantomime. . . ." She hummed along, pausing now and then to receive a low remark from Mrs. Joplin, who was definitely, she decided, the perfect wife for a minister. Particularly the *worried* sort of minister that Dr. Joplin appeared to be, because even in a room of people *quite* unrelated to his mission he had that sort of flocky look. Mrs. Joplin was a natural coper, you could tell at a glance, the just-leave-it-all-to-me sort. Mrs. Gibson, who never tried to cope at all, was filled with honest admiration.

Glancing up, she saw, with relief, Mr. Hartwig take his departure from the room. Really, the old man was a walking remonstrance. His whole spirit seemed bent by the loss of his livery. It was making Mrs. Gibson sad.

Wally, in the window seat, was being tentative about looking at Gretchen. He'd been a little afraid to see her. More than anything, he wanted to keep the glowing security Nelle brought him, but he'd been away from Gretchen before. Each time, the moment of remeeting had been disastrous, from his angle. Nothing could be more obvious than Gretchen's fond indifference. Nothing, till lately, had been more heartbreaking. He looked at her deliberately. Beautiful Gretchen, in claret silk, her hair in a low thick knot. And he looked away. In time, he thought, it will be easier. He'd never believed in loves that last through years of unrequition—if there was such a word. Of course, he'd been rather hopelessly loving Gretchen for a long time now, but. . . . He looked at her again. The smartest thing to do, he decided, is stay away from her. Because lately, with Nelle, he'd actually forgotten to think of Gretchen at all for hours at a time.

Beside him, and warmly in his thoughts, was Nelle. He mused, in a typically Wally way, that Nelle was like good tweed or linen—the imperfections were there to see, and without the

185

imperfections it wouldn't be good tweed or linen. That seemed to him quite fair as analysis, but questionable as a compliment. The sort of thing that Gretchen used to laugh at. I must stop, he decided, thinking *"used to."* It's a terribly sad phrase . . . like *"long ago."*

In the fashion of dinner parties, this one showed a tendency to group itself, with Mrs. Gibson a sort of wandering messenger between. Wally, listening to her pleasant skimming voice swirl round the reticent Mrs. Joplin, wondered if the agreeable but almost totally silent Archer didn't sometimes long for just one real line of sense from his wife. Probably not. Probably the surprise of it would be too unsettling.

"Oh, Wally," said the present woman of his thoughts, "what in the world are you doing, sitting in the window like a plant?"

"He's probably studying us," Nelle said.

"Are you, Wally? How unkind. Ah, here is Dr. Joplin. Dr. Joplin, this is Wally Chase of whom you've heard so much. Wally's so facinated by—the Egyptians, isn't it, Wally? Something, anyway, you'll have in common."

Dr. Joplin, who had not heard so much of Wally, nothing at all in fact, and who already met him at dinner, said how do you do, and ah, yes, the Egyptians, as Mrs. Gibson flowed away toward Kenneth and Rosemary, now sitting with Mrs. Bemis.

Funny, Wally thought, listening to Dr. Joplin and looking at Nelle, how the hostess really sets the tone of a party. Mrs. Gibson's could be nothing but this . . . fine food, light talk, and many shiftings. Everyone having a pretty evening in a detached and mindless manner. He wondered, with amusement, what Mrs. Bemis was making of it.

"I envy you your leisure, and your pursuits," Dr. Joplin was saying, staring about beatifically. Dr. Joplin was incapable of commanding his expression, and it gave his wife, across the room, great pleasure to see him blinking blissfully at young Mr. Chase because she knew his inner feelings to be accurately recorded. Dr. Grafton had helped more people than Rosemary, Mrs. Joplin concluded. "Aside from Biblical history, Mr. Chase," Dr. Joplin was saying, "I know little of the Egyptian people, except, of course, a smattering of the Ptolemies, those great princes of learning. One of them, I believe, caused a translation of the Old Testament to be made into Greek during his reign?" Actually Dr. Joplin knew much more than he professed, but proceeded on the theory that most people prefer to impart, rather than share, knowledge.

Wally warmed. He adored instructing. "That's it. Ptolemy Philadelphus. He had seventy scholars labor day and night on the translation. He was Ptolemaeus II, you know. All of them, down to his son, were great patrons of learning, and very excellent rulers, but the family sort of went to pieces after that. Philadelphus increased the famous library to something like two hundred thousand volumes. A great part of it burned, of course, by Caesar's fleet. Not that Caesar ever said anything about it," he went on with bitterness over the loss of books nearly three hundred years before Christ.

Dr. Joplin listened eagerly. Nelle hugged her happiness at Wally's brightening face. Oh, Gretchen can say anything she wants, Nelle sang inwardly. Call him a pedant, imply he's a bore. But he's wonderful. It's so marvelous to see someone caring so for something that isn't oilcloth or glacé gloves from Paris.

Rosemary sat silent on a huge grey hassock, as Gretchen and her mother talked with Kenneth, and Mrs. Gibson reappeared with the smiling suddenness of the Cheshire cat. She sat silent, and when there was a chance, studied Kenneth's fine face, considered the perfections of his mind, the warmth of his concern. She wondered if without him she'd be what she was now, a nearly peaceful person with all sorts of plans. Probably not, she decided, though it might have come later. But there must be a time in nearly everyone's life when it's impossible to go on without help. I was lucky, she thought, because I got help when I needed it most.

"Gretchen tells me you may come out to Indiana later in the summer, Rosemary," Mrs. Bemis said.

"Oh. Oh yes, we were speaking of it, and I'd love to. There's something I have to work out first . . . a sort of plan," she said slowly. Kenneth looked up with interest but said nothing.

"Well, anytime at all will be fine," Mrs. Bemis assured her. "I think the rest of the family will be all packed when we get back. We get awfully restless about this time. . . ."

Gretchen, remembering the spice of pine and balsam and current bushes warm in the sun; flight of the hasty dragonflies over wrinkling water to weightless perches on the broad lily pads; the cobwebbed mist of the morning and transparent dark of night; remembering this, and the shouting laughter of William and Noah, the darting sprite that was Pru in levis on her way to a horse; remembering, in a weaving of pictures all that was summer in Indiana, closed her eyes against a longing so intense, and, closing them, saw Orin Whitney. She seemed, lately, to *feel* so much. Nothing was partly . . . it was all utter, and whole, and sharp. Desire for summer, for yet another word from the dark Whitney, for something hidden but springing in her own life, her own being. Where was the source of this leaping awareness? Gretchen, with a little rush of held breath, opened her eyes, looked straight in the eyes of Mr. Hartwig, wistful and denied in the doorway.

"Why," she asked suddenly, "is your butler so sad?" It was important to know.

Mrs. Gibson sighed deeply. "Because he's deprived."

"Deprived?"

"Of magic," said Mrs. Gibson, who would have surprised Wally and Mrs. Bemis, but not Archer, with her swift though infrequent glances of comprehension. She rose, went to Mr. Hartwig, drew him into the hall.

"Mr. Hartwig," she said, "I was wrong. Would you like to see the guests out at the door in your costume?" At his expression, she amended hastily, "In your livery?"

Later, each departing guest was startled and greatly impressed by Mr. Hartwig's radiant attendance to their exits. There was no question—he cut a stunning figure at the last.

Chapter 16.

MRS. BEMIS sat at her high window in the hotel room, looking down at Central Park. She was glad she'd decided to stay the four days of her visit in New York. Gretchen, the most exquisite understander, had agreed immediately. She'd be working, anyway, she said, and could easily get in to visit her mother when there was time. Oddly enough, there had been more trouble with Mrs. Gibson, who had pronounced herself simply shattered that Mrs. Bemis wouldn't stay at her home.

"I'll even," Mrs. Gibson had said with an air of producing trump, "I'll even remove May's sequinned screen from the guest room. Only, if you run into her, do say casually how impressive it is. And it *is*," she'd added moodily. "Nelle had a simple brainstorm when she took May to the Museum to see some pots they have down there. Now May is going to Mexico to study under a pottier, if there is such a thing? Well, a master potmaker, and it *is* such a relief not to have to think about tearooms any more. But she isn't going till next week, so if you do meet, I suppose we should have her over for tea because I know she'd love to meet Gretchen's . . ." She'd gone on, and Mrs. Bemis had been in despair of getting a word in, or herself out. But she had, by exercising exasperated tact, and here she was, high above the city, safe from the kindly, maddening conversation of Mrs. Archer Gibson.

On Central Park Lake, traditional sailors oared lazily in traditional rowboats, their tiny circling craft looking, from this distance, like floating toys. From the zoo came the bark of the sea lions, and straight beneath her window the floor of the canyon, Fifth Avenue, skirled and skittered and ran. From under an archway of light-dappled branches, two horsemen trotted, little dancing centaurs. Mrs. Bemis thought of Prudence, as one must always, she admitted with a half-regretful smile, think of Prudence at the appearance of horse. She did sometimes wish it could be slightly otherwise. But that, she thought, is the quality of youth. It *is* youth, that ardent all-occupying ability to enjoy and to anticipate. The pity of growing up, of growing old, she thought now, is not that your frame grows weary and demanding, not that your children slip from your side. The pity is that your own thoughts cease to astonish, your own desires cease to matter much. Or, perhaps, that your future was gone. That brilliant, never-coming, adored and certain triumph, your future, no longer existed.

But is it a pity, she wondered, turning into the room, midway between laughter and sadness, that once you no longer have it, you wouldn't take it as a gift?

The telephone squealed.

"Mother?" Gretchen said. "Rosemary and I are down here. We want to shop for things and have lunch at Schrafft's and we want you with us. Shall we come up or will you come down?"

"I'll be there. I'll be with you in a minute." She hung up, reached for her new straw hat, humming as she stood before the mirror to adjust it. No, she thought, when you are my age, you wouldn't take the future for a gift. But the present can be flawless when it comes by itself.

The hotel corridor, muffled in broadloom, silence, and closed doors, was empty as she walked to the elevator. Mrs. Bemis loved hotels. They were so unreal, so artfully subservient, so expensive. Four days in a hotel is a delicious experience, she thought, stepping aboard, eying an elegant card on the elevator wall—well-known chanteuse, glimpse of her shoulder and profile, her name in a flung spray of golden script. On silken cables the car streamed downward, doors whispered open, and the glowing Gothic lobby was at her feet. She shivered a little, realizing that some people lived in this truthless enchantment all the time.

Gretchen and Rosemary were at a jeweler's showcase, mesmerized by a sapphire on velvet. They looked, thought Mrs. Bemis, utterly charming. Gretchen, beautiful and poised as a young deer. Rosemary, with her brushed fair hair, her face a treasure, her eyes alight, as if they had just begun to see. She had remembered Rosemary as the most disturbing little figure, large-eyed and hesitant, with a child's way of averting her gaze. There was still, in this alert, secure girl, a trace of that poor little ghost. A trace, no doubt, that would never leave. Mrs. Bemis thought it just as well. She believed that childhood's fears and sorrows should linger in some part to temper those which come later. For how, she wondered, could we stand the shock of loss or terror if each time it came afresh?

They turned from the sapphire at her approach.

"Having now seen what we cannot buy," Gretchen said, "let's go find what we can."

"What are you shopping for?" Mrs. Bemis asked.

"Oh, stuff. White nylons, a few little presents for this one and that. All things we could buy just as easily without coming to New York, only it's fun."

They went through revolving doors, onto the bright pavements in which winking bits of mica caught and reflected the sun. Up and down the Avenue went the people. Women bobbing like bright balloons, arrested, swaying, before the dazzling snares of shop windows. Drifting on. Luncheon? Oh, where? Sling pumps and butterfly pins and lobster bisque and lingerie. Charge it, enlarge it, store it till fall. Then on, on down the Avenue. . . . The men, firm-footed, walked where they were going straight till they got there. This is all very serious, I'm very important, nothing can start till I'm there, out of my way please, I'm in an important hurry, said the men's firm feet on the pavement.

Mrs. Bemis and the two girls drifted, ensnared here and there by the shop windows. Papier-maché unicorn prancing on spindrift of blue gauze—but what in the world was he to sell? Oh yes, the little flagon of perfume speared on the tip of his pearl horn. A ballet girl, tip toe, slender arms crooked above her head, silver dress glinting behind glass. And what did she. . . . She wore slippers, called *Giselles,* to be found in Better Shoes, Fourth Floor. The card that said so was very discreet and small and it looked like a theatre program.

The luggage was cream-colored, amber-handled, magnificent.

"Anywhere but on the Queen Mary you'd look like a fool," Gretchen said.

The walls were rose satin, encrusted with lace.

"It's a candy store," Rosemary explained.

The stone martens were looped through a diamond tiara.

"Of course not, but is it all right if I look at them?" said Mrs. Bemis.

Gretchen and Rosemary bought two pair of white nylons apiece. Gretchen bought three large silk squares. "You'll get one, Rosemary, so you might as well pick the one you like." Rosemary, after wondering from shop to shop, bought a silver chain with four dangling lipsticks, an Irish linen handkerchief, and something she didn't let Gretchen see.

Mrs. Bemis treated to lunch. "Let's go to one of those places where you sit on the sidewalk under an awning."

"Well, all right," Gretchen said dubiously.

"Why, don't you like them?"

"They look pretty in the pictures and from across the street, but somehow when you get there it's always sort of gritty, isn't it, Rosemary?"

" 'Fraid so," said Rosemary.

They went to Schrafft's.

Over salad and iced tea and little hot rolls, they considered the beauty and the appalling expense of the market place. Mrs. Bemis said it was a form of masochism even to walk through the pastel, perfumed temples that were upper Fifth Avenue department stores. Some of the dresses had names, like "*Dream of Me*," or, "*Scandalous One*." Oh well, she sighed, captured, as any woman is, irrespective of her own measurements, by the sort of dress that "*Dream of Me*" had been.

"Don't you have to be on duty, Rosemary?" she asked, turning a broad firm back on fantasy.

"I'll have time if I catch the 1:05. That's why we asked to eat so early."

"Oh, is that it. I thought you were both starving."

"That's Rosemary, not me," Gretchen said quickly, feeling her appetite was too much remarked. "Do you realize that the day after tomorrow, at this time, we'll be getting ready to graduate?"

"Realize?" Rosemary wailed. "I get weary in the knees and stomach just thinking of it."

"How nice it is to know you'll be coming out to us soon," Mrs. Bemis said. "I just know you'll enjoy it, and the children would love having you."

"Mother's always calling us the children," Gretchen said, shaking her head. "For myself, I don't mind. But it drives Hally wild."

"If you haven't changed your minds," Rosemary said suddenly, "I'd like to come soon. Not when you do, but next week, if I can get ready."

"Why'd, that'd be marvelous," Gretchen said. She almost, not quite, asked what had changed Rosemary's mind. Nelle's continued evasiveness had given her a rather upsetting lesson in the evils of interfering.

In any case, Rosemary did not want to explain just then. What her plan was she wished first to tell Kenneth, then her parents. Young plans, like young plants, thrive best if protected.

"Maybe you could fly out," Gretchen went on. "Mother flew, and she loved it, didn't you?"

"Not quite," said Mrs. Bemis. "But it was really very good traveling." She smiled. "Mrs. Gibson was astonished to hear I flew. 'It's too *harrowing* just seeing people off, like saying good-by forever, not a bit like a boat or a train and no fruit of course....'"

Rosemary giggled, but Gretchen frowned. "Mother," she explained, "does this sort of thing because she's a good mimic. Sometimes it isn't polite."

"Oh, darling," Mrs. Bemis apologized, "I'm sorry, truly. But I didn't feel impolite. She's such a remarkable woman, no one could help quoting her."

"My stepmother was very happy to meet you," Rosemary said, staring absently at the luncheon remains. And then, "Thanks awfully for the lunch and for asking me out there. I have to pop if I'm going to make that train. I'll see you at graduation, won't I?" She gathered purse, gloves, packages, and ran.

Mrs. Bemis looked after the light figure with its rippling yellow hair, then turned back to her daughter. "Gretchen, what's changed her? She's so much more...."

"Isn't she though?" Gretchen said when her mother broke off. "I think basically she changed herself. She might have even without Dr. Grafton's help, which is a good thing. But she got

195

very ill, and Dr. Grafton who's an embryo psychiatrist—good, too—just happened to be there at the right time. He likes Rosemary, I guess," she concluded.

"She's a different person. Is she in love, then?"

"No, I don't think so. Not yet, anyway," Gretchen said with a great sigh.

If Gretchen were not my daughter, Mrs. Bemis thought, if I had not known her eyes and her voice for years, I'd never guess that something was troubling her. And if she were not Gretchen, I wouldn't have the sense to be quiet. I can wait and be quiet because I know what will happen. Some evening, some morning, when she feels sure of what she wants to say, Gretchen will talk to me. And then I may be able to help. Her eyes strayed around the dining room. It was nearly filled with women. Here and there a man, looking like a duffle bag at a fashion show.

Gretchen, following her mother's glance, nodded. "The strongest man," she said sympathetically, "is nothing but a cipher in a Fifth Avenue Schrafft's at noon. I sometimes wonder why they do it. Shall we go?"

That evening, Kenneth was waiting for Rosemary as she came off duty. It was her last night. Tomorrow the seniors would not work, next day they'd graduate. She went down the hall, past the darkened X-ray rooms, locked clinic doors, past Emergency, brilliantly alight and empty save for a graduate checking equipment. Around the corner, through a door, into the warm night watered with moonlight.

Kenneth perched on the low iron fence. He threw away a cigarette and stood up as she approached, and they walked along the moonlit gravel path to the little stone bench by the gold-fish pond. Rosemary folded her hands in her lap, Kenneth laced strong fingers around one knee, and they sat in the silence.

The clear dark waters of the pond were smooth and still. Shapes of gold and silver suspended over the sandy bottom. The garden, softly asleep, breathed the faintest dreaming fragrance, and overhead the moon, a large speckled nutmeg, gleamed amid the stars.

"You're feeling better, aren't you, Rosemary?" Kenneth said.

"Oh, I am, Kenneth. I feel . . . conquering."

"That's fine."

Silence closed over them again, and beyond it, as through a wall of darkness, came the voice of the hospital. Kenneth had a nice smell, of soap and antiseptic and clean starched clothes.

"You know," he began.

"Yes, Kenneth?"

"You know, I got a kick out of that butler of Mrs. Gibson's. I'm glad she let him wear that rig at last. He was just about ready to cry, Mrs. Gibson said."

"Poor man."

"He'd borrowed it from a strolling minstrel or something. Nice old fellow, he was."

"Mmm. . . ."

Kenneth rubbed a hand over his chin. It rasped a bit.

"You need a shave," Rosemary said.

"Guess I do."

"Kenneth," she said, turning to him abruptly, her voice so charged with the tone that means the words to come will be precious and important that he began to share her smile even before she told him—"Kenneth, I'm going in the Army."

His smile faded slowly. After a moment, he said curiously, "Do you know what you'll be doing, Rosemary?"

"Why, Kenneth, I thought you'd be pleased." Her voice still brimmed with triumph. Kenneth's reluctance to share it was apparently not going to affect her. It crossed his mind that no sign she'd showed so far had been more auspicious. Rosemary

197

was discovering that she had feet to stand on and a mind to make up. He noticed something else too. That the vitality Dolph had said she lacked was not lacking any more. It makes her very pretty, he decided.

"Well, for a girl who disliked Emergency, you've picked a rather rough road," was his comment.

"*The road to Damascus is a rocky one and long,*" she quoted, as one who is quite prepared to travel it.

"When did all this happen?"

"Well—," she hesitated, and then laughed. "Actually it hasn't happened at all."

"Rosemary, what are you talking about?"

"The Army, Kenneth, the Army."

Kenneth waited.

"Oh, all right. I'll be sensible. Now—I went down to 90 Church Street, in New York, and I applied for a second lieutenant's commission in the Army. But of course they said I had to graduate and pass the state boards first. So then I went to Miss Merkle, to see if she'd give me—a good record. Not on work, I know that's all right. On—personality. And she said she saw no reason why I shouldn't make a good Army nurse, and she'd say so in writing. So—I'm as good as in, wouldn't you say?"

"Well, no," said Kenneth, laughing.

"Don't be a stick. I thought I'd tell you before telling my parents. You being my—Pygmalion?—as it were. Now, aren't you pleased?"

Kenneth said he was more than pleased, he was proud. He said he'd take her out to dinner to celebrate. He didn't mention what had pleased him most about the entire conversation—that quite unconsciously Rosemary had referred to her "parents." Not to "my father and Mrs. Joplin." She'll be all right, he told himself. A very gratifying first patient.

Chapter 17.

THE next day, Preston and Dr. Whitney played their last game of tennis.

Orin Whitney had wrested an hour out of his busy afternoon and appeared at the courts as Preston finished setting up the net.

"Timed it just right, doctor," he greeted.

"That's how I meant it to be," Whitney replied imperturbably.

They volleyed, Dr. Whitney won the serve, and sent it booming to the edge of the court. Preston, with a gleeful smile, was on his way at the swing of the doctor's racket. He ran back and sideways, arched, and crumpled in an oddly small heap on the ground.

For a fraction of a second, Dr. Whitney, poised for the return, stood still as stone. Then he cleared the net and was at Preston's side, kneeling with an anguished face over his friend.

Dorry Palmer entered Gretchen's room without knocking. "Gosh," she squealed before she was fairly in. "Isn't it awful about Preston?"

Gretchen dropped her hair brush. "What do you mean, awful about Preston? What's wrong with Preston?"

"Didn't you hear?" Dorry exclaimed, obviously delighted to be the first with bad news. "He and Dr. Whitney—oh boy, that Whitney—well, they were playing tennis early this afternoon. . . ."

"Look, will you get on with it?" Gretchen said impatiently.

Dorry blinked. "Well, I like that. Here I come to tell you something I thought you'd be interested in, and all you do is growl. What I say is. . . ." But Gretchen hadn't waited to hear what Dorry would say. Pinning up her hair as she ran down the hall, she caught a departing elevator.

"What's happened to Preston?" she asked the operator.

He turned with a puzzled look. "Heart attack, Miss Bemis. Gee, he's so young. . . ."

"Is he. . . ." She swallowed, unable to continue.

"Oh, no, Miss Bemis. Thank God, no. They've got him in a private room—Dr. Whitney's expense, they say—and they say the doctor's like a wild man. He and Preston are sure good friends."

"It isn't only that," Gretchen said, mostly to herself. "Thanks. I'll let you know what. . . ."

"Do that, will you, Miss Bemis? Preston's a great guy. I'd sure hate to see anything happen to him."

Something already has, Gretchen thought. But she went on quickly. Well, this'll do it, she thought. I bet anything this will do it. Mr. Whitney said it would take a real jolt.

She encountered Miss Merkle just outside the Director's office.

"Oh, there you are, Gretchen," Miss Merkle said. Neither of them noticed she'd used Gretchen's first name, which she'd never done before. "You've heard about Preston." It wasn't a question.

Gretchen nodded.

Miss Merkle turned toward the office. "Well—we'll have to have our conference anyway. This is. . . . Oh, dear."

"Conference?" Gretchen said blankly. And then, "Oh, yes. I'd forgotten."

"You're the last one. Actually I just wanted to talk to you, because you'll know without my help what you want to do. Sit down, won't you?"

Gretchen dropped to a chair. "Miss Merkle. How bad is he?"

"He's conscious. He reacted to the stimulants."

"Could I special him? Please. I would really like to. I'd go home later. . . ."

"You're very good, Gretchen. No, Dr. Whitney's already engaged three nurses. He's pretty upset, I'm afraid."

Gretchen said nothing. Not her province to discuss Dr. Whitney. Miss Merkle didn't mean her to. It had been a chance remark, just to be saying something, to try to talk a sorrow away. For a while no further remark was made. They sat there, brooding, thinking of Preston's vigorous body lying without motion on a bed upstairs. And what of his mind? Gretchen wondered. What of the shock and the terror in Preston's fine brain? "It must be so terrible," she said slowly, "So terrible to lie there, knowing whatever happens, you aren't the same, you'll never be the same again."

Miss Merkle said none of the foolish things. Not that everything would straighten out, that he'd live to be ninety, that he'd be just like everybody else. She said, "Well, he's Preston. And that's a help."

They talked then, without spirit, of Gretchen's plans to go to college and enter Public Health.

"You'll be good there," Miss Merkle said. "Dr. Bradley said she hoped you would go ahead with it."

"She's been—very nice to me. Oh gosh, Miss Merkle, I just can't talk about it now. I feel so—so sick and useless."

Briefly, Miss Merkle put her head in her hands. "That's all

201

most of us can do, when someone we care for is hurt. Just feel sick and useless. Sometimes I almost forget what death and illness are, I see so much of it. It's something like this that makes it real again. Awfully real," she said, lifting her head, staring into the hall. She rose a little in her chair, "There's. . . . Oh, Doctor," she called, coming quickly around the desk. "Doctor, is there anything you could tell us?"

Dr. Whitney, still in white tennis clothes, walked slowly into the office. He nodded to Gretchen, who had risen, her eyes fixed on his face.

Dr. Whitney said without expression, "He's sleeping. He'll have to be in bed for several weeks, and then I just don't know what he'll do." His voice was rough with pain and anger, but as he turned to go, he looked back, as though for something he'd forgotten. "Oh. May I take Miss Bemis along? I'd like to talk to her."

"Of course, Doctor," Miss Merkle said, curious but polite. "We've finished for the present."

Gretchen glanced thankfully at Miss Merkle and left with Dr. Whitney. They walked out of the building. On the white lines of the tennis courts, lines newly laid by Preston, the sinking sun shone brilliantly. All around, as far as they could see, the trim lawns and springing flowers spoke of Preston's hand and skill. The full-leaved beeches and willows and maples stirred in the twilight breeze, and birds in feathered dartings sang about being sleepy.

Dr. Whitney went out on the court to retrieve two fallen rackets. Carefully he drew on the covers, screwed the presses. He pushed them under his arm and walked along, looking once to be sure Gretchen was with him.

"Have you anything to do?" he said finally.

"No. Nothing right away."

"Come for a drive with me?"

Gretchen nodded, unable to say a word, unable to press down a wild sweet surge of happiness. She was sad with everything in her for Preston, but bliss rose, and she could not stop it, her love stronger than loyalty or conscience, stronger than herself.

They drove slowly up the hill beyond town to a hilltop over the river. The round cherry-red sun sank quickly into the purple-wooded Palisades, and day, not alight, not dark, drained peacefully out of the sky.

Dr. Whitney lit a cigarette for himself, then with a half-worded apology, one for Gretchen. His fingers barely brushing hers set her hand trembling. And, oh, I love you so much, she said silently. I'm so much in love with you.

"Gretchen," he began, and then stopped. He didn't notice either having said her name. It's strange, she thought, how easily something important shreds away formality. She waited with no sense of waiting. She'd have sat in silence the rest of her life for whatever he wanted to say. After a while he went on. "Gretchen, I guess now I'll do it—give up the practice and try to go back a few years. I'm going to try for the place in Long Island, but one way or another, I'm going into research. It's too bad it took—this—to get me started. But I won't change my mind again."

"Preston will be glad," Gretchen said softly.

He smiled a little. "I was glad to see you there in the office."

It just isn't possible, Gretchen thought, nobody can be this happy. She was afraid to look at him, for fear so much happiness must show in her eyes. He was sad and hurt and angry, and he had to be. Preston was his friend. But I'm sad, too, she cried within. Only I'm in love, and it seems to make everything different.

Dr. Whitney was slipping his hands up and down on the smooth thick steering wheel, tightening his fists now and then, relaxing them hopelessly, over and over. Gretchen wanted to ask him something, but she wouldn't say Orin, and if she said Dr. Whitney, he might call her Miss Bemis again. So she had either to tap his arm or wait for him to look at her. She waited, and in a little while he turned.

Once before their glances had met and held, with a sort of surprise, a sort of meeting. And now again it was there, the soft unspoken question, an awareness between them, and everything in her forbid him to look away, or to think, for this moment, of anything but the two of them and a question that had an answer in their eyes.

The answer, for Orin Whitney, had an element of disbelief. He'd seen this girl for, what was it, three years now? And only in the past few weeks had he noticed or cared that her voice was low, her words soothing, her face very beautiful indeed. Dr. Whitney, the least rash of people, was not ready to believe it. He held his tongue and looked away, quite unaware that he'd already answered the question without speaking.

Gretchen sighed softly as he put the car in gear. "When will you know, about the appointment?" she asked when they were driving slowly through the darkening night toward the hospital, now alight.

"I don't know. I'll call a couple of people and write some letters. It won't be quick, in any case. It's peculiar, but now that I've made up my mind, I don't feel impatient any more. I'd have to see Preston through this, no matter what else happens."

"Isn't there anything he'll be able to do? That you can think of, I mean?"

"Oh, yes. I was just—angry—back there. He'll be able to go on with his flowers and trees. Not the hardest part of course—no more rolling the courts. . . ." He accelerated abruptly. "I ought to get back."

Gretchen felt a touch of panic. This man had such a way of

taking off without a word, and in two days she'd be taking off herself. He might forget, in the confusion that would surely descend on him now, that he'd ever answered wordlessly a question they had shared. He doesn't, she realized a bit frantically, even know he did. And if his days become too full, he may never find a moment to think and understand. The wheels turned, every turn brought them closer to parting, and Gretchen could think of nothing to say, no way to fan the little flame that had flickered into being. Words tumbled through her mind without meaning. She sat in despair as the car nosed into the doctors' parking area. She thought, *there is still time, still time.* And now there was not. He was Dr. Whitney once again, on his ground, bound for a patient. Any word now would be futile. Anything but, "Good-by, Dr. Whitney. I hope Preston will—will be all right."

He walked beside her, abstracted. "Yes," he said remotely. "Let's hope so." With a sideways glance, "Thanks, Miss Bemis. You're very—restful."

"I'm glad if I help."

Caught back, he studied her face. "You do," he said. "More than I can say." He seemed for a moment to know that there was something more—to say, or to do. She could feel the words gathering behind his silence. But they didn't come.

The moment was swift, Gretchen helpless, and he was gone through the wide open doors with everything left not done. It's hard to be a girl, she thought, to sit around waiting, hoping, smiling the gallant smile while nothing gets done about you.

Her mother was waiting in the lounge of the Residence, and they went in to dinner.

Graduation Day dawned warm and blue. Gretchen went over early to see Preston on the Fifth Floor private wing. As she stepped out of the elevator, every bell, loud-speaker and nurse in the place seemed to begin shouting for Harold, the porter. "Calling Harold," said the speaker at this end; "Harold," the speaker at that end; "Harold," the nurse at the desk called as a doctor looked out a door and said "Harold, come here, will you."

Harold, going down the hall, stopped in his tracks, moving his head around toward each summons as it came. He gave Gretchen a slanting smile, and "*Figaro!*" he laughed, and went toward the desk.

Gretchen smiled after him, then went on. There was Harold, working all the time, she'd heard. But he usually looked cheery, enjoyed people and things. He almost had to find pleasure in each day as it passed, having no days set aside in which to concentrate on it, no vacations to look forward to and say, well I'm not having a good time now, but oh boy, when my vacation comes . . . .

Mrs. Wold, the morning special, met her at the door of Preston's room. "Oh good, Miss Bemis," she said. "You wouldn't mind staying here a moment while I run down to the pharmacy, would you?"

"Not at all. How is he?"

Mrs. Wold nodded. "Doing nicely," she said, hurrying off.

Preston, propped against many pillows, was watching the assistant gardener run the little red tractor over the lawns. Through the open window came the soft putt-puttings of grassy progress.

He turned as Gretchen came in "Nice day for you," he said, and smiled his pleasure at seeing her.

Gretchen sat in an aggressively gay chair, watching his face for signs of terror or protest there. It seemed inconceivable, but Preston, aside from the strangeness of seeing him in bed, was just Preston. Deep eyes fatigued, thin face drawn and pale beneath the tan, but Preston still. Calm and reassuring against his pillows, commenting on the weather. She thought it was wonderful for him to be so—so mental, so peaceful, so—passionless. But it wouldn't, she told herself, be wonderful for everyone. Not at all wonderful for me.

"You are doing well, aren't you?" she said with relief.

He nodded. "Orin says so."

They accepted that together as the ultimate reassurance.

Preston's room overlooked the front of the hospital. From his window they could see the circular driveway, abutted by a grey stone wall, the wide entrance doors, the green lawns, and the town beyond. Gretchen moved over to the window, perching on the sill. She looked at the town, tumbled uphill and down, at a weathercock glinting gold atop the Civic Building, at the red and yellow trolley laboring past down the street. People crossed, recrossed, with children, bundles, with reluctant dogs. Doors closed behind them. They opened windows to look out. They walked up steps and around corners.

That's the world, Gretchen thought. That vigorous, disordered, living patch of town. Take it over and over and it's the world. Oh, world—I'm not sure I wish to take you even once, far less over and over.

"Confusing," she commented.

A hugely impressive car purred sedately up the drive to the front door. Mrs. A. Dexter Smalling, several other Board members, and an apprehensive but resolute Miss Merkle, converged on the limousine as the chauffeur swept the door back to reveal its contents. The gentleman who emerged, a prosperous type, received an accolade from Mrs. Smalling and satellites with the patient geniality of one who must, in the nature of things, receive accolades. He lifted a wry brow to this one, nodded gravely to that, and turning his head with happy impartiality was borne into the hospital. The chauffeur climbed back in the car and wheeled soundlessly off.

"Guest speaker," Gretchen decided.

"I wonder what *he'll* talk about."

"The threshold of life—what else? First, he'll be waggish, very delicately waggish, to put us at our ease. Then he'll sweep the assemblage, his gaze grown sober, and after a moment of throbbing silence, he'll say, 'The Threshold of Life.' And he'll say it half a dozen times, interspersed with 'great privilege,' 'highest duty,' and 'service to,' etc."

"Don't forget the cool hands and the flushed brow."

"Do you really think he will?" Gretchen asked with pleasure. "Well, let's hope so. If they had any sense, of course, they'd have Miss Merkle speak. Or Dr. Bradley. Someone who knows. I wonder why it's always someone like him," she said, tilting her head toward the empty doorway.

"He's probably threatening to leave them some money," Preston said. "That always puts an institution at a disadvantage."

She gazed over the town, disclaiming any connection between themselves and the opulent stranger.

"I am waiting," Gretchen said at length, "for you to ask me whether I know what I'm going to do."

Preston smiled. "I knew you'd say when you got around to it."

Gretchen looked at and away from the image of Orin Whitney, always with her now. What she was going to do, it seemed, had nothing to do with him. "I'm going back to college, and then into Public Health."

Preston nodded. A slow, thoughtful gesture. "I think that's the right thing for you." The urge in Gretchen to give, he mused, would surely be more satisfied in giving her skill, her courage, really, than in giving, as she had in the past, so many—things.

"Are you getting tired?" Gretchen asked, realizing that she'd been there quite a while.

"Oh, no, I like having you here." But he seemed to lean more heavily against his pillows. Gretchen rearranged them for him. "You'll be missing your lunch," he commented.

"You may doubt this, but I don't want any. I'm going now, but not to lunch. I'm going up to my room and gloat over my flowers and weep a little for the years that will never come back." Why is it, she thought, why should it be that when we most mean something, we must speak lightly. Because she would surely weep, she could feel the waiting tears, for the years, for the people, for a girl called Gretchen that she'd never know again.

Preston's long glance understood all this, but he didn't speak.

Mrs. Wold, returning from the basement pharmacy, said that Gretchen had better go now. "But thanks for staying," she added as she drove Gretchen toward the door.

Gretchen looked at Preston with concern.

"Don't fuss," he reassured her. "I'm not tired. Graduate happily and come in again, won't you?"

"You know I will, Preston."

Graduation ceremonies were to begin at three o'clock. At one-thirty, Murphy came down the hall, knocked at Gretchen's door. "Phone for Bemis," she called and went on.

Gretchen had been removing Emmett Kelly from the wall, holding him carefully to flick the dust away. "Oh, thanks," she called at Murphy's message, laying Mr. Kelly carefully on her bed.

"Hello?" she said, slightly breathless at the phone.

"Gretchen? Miss Bemis? This is Orin Whitney."

Oh, I know, I know, you don't have to tell me, Dr. Whitney, she sang, closing her eyes in an upwhirling joy. "Yes, Dr. Whitney...."

"Look here, Preston just told me you're graduating today. I thought something must be going on; place looks like Pimlico. Only why didn't you tell me?"

"Why I. . . . It just didn't seem like a good time, yesterday. I mean, you had so much on your mind and all."

"Well, besides the 'and all,' I seem to have you on it too. So could you. . . . Ooops, excuse me. . . . Say, Gretchen, can you hustle down here and see me a minute before I trip anyone else up?"

For a second she just smiled at the telephone. Dear, beautiful, black little darling of a telephone. She caressed it with her eyes.

"Are you there, Gretchen?" His voice was harried. Behind it, she could hear the beelike chorus of the voices of many friends and relations.

"Yes, I'm here. I'll be there. You're right downstairs?"

"You'll find me in the throngs. Hurry, won't you?"

"I'll hurry."

Dr. Whitney, in the Nurses' Residence. It was really sensational. For me, for me—he's waiting down there for me, she caroled, speeding down the hall to the assurance of her mirror. She looked all right. She looked like a rocket about to go off.

Downstairs, she didn't see him at first. She saw a brilliant molten mass of gowns and summer suits, topped by myriad moving hats, borne up on a current of sound. The visitors, the proud spectators. Probably she knew many of them. Deliberately, she singled out no faces but moved blankly through the throng. When she saw the one dark face, the one tall figure, her vision would clear.

"Gretchen. . . ."

Beside her then. Not smiling, but looking down in her eyes with the sense of their questions asked, answered. It's you, he said, though his words were only, "Can't we find a place with less than a thousand people in it?"

210

I'm bewitched, thought Gretchen. No—I'm loved.

"Perhaps the little lecture room," she told him.

Mercifully, the little lecture room was unoccupied. He closed the door and stood, very close to her, watching her. Had she wanted to, Gretchen could have kept nothing from her lifted glance. It took—for a moment—his breath away. What an incredible, what a terrifying thing, to make another person look so transfigured with happiness.

"Do I look like that?" he asked her.

She nodded. "You look. . . . Yes, you do."

"I love you, Gretchen."

"I love you." Her voice was dreamy, and she swayed a little forward. But there was no dreaminess in Orin Whitney. His arms around her were hard, as she had known they would be, and his kiss alive and urgent.

In a little while he spoke, still holding her close, so that she could feel his low voice as she heard it.

"Gretchen, Gretchen. . ." he said. "I didn't know it would be like this. All the time—before—I thought it was something else. Something other people had . . . thought they had. I just didn't know," he said again, moving his cheek against hers, as though to be sure how near she was. His voice was very sure now, very strong. But all the reticence that was Dr. Whitney had gone, and, for her, all the love that was Orin filled his words. "You're very lovely," he said softly. "Will you marry me, Gretchen?"

Gretchen, in his arms, gave him his answer without a word.

At a little past two o'clock, the visitors who had swarmed upstairs and down were in the auditorium. The senior graduating nurses were in their rooms, shyly closeted with their first white uniforms, thinking it won't be long now. . . .

Voices in the hall rang and crossed.

"Please, somebody please, tell me where this thing buttons."

"Should we carry our scissors?"

"Well, didn't you ask? Ask somebody. . . ."

"What about you, Palmer? What are you going to do?"

"Oh, didn't you hear about Dorry? She's going to Chock-chick-wahoo in the beautiful Berkshires and put band-aids on little girls' bee bites."

"Band-aids on bee bites? Was it for this we labored so long?"

"Did you hear Murphy has a date with Dr. Horner?"

"It's a fluke. We looked at each other so long in Emergency that he finally asked me in order to fill a nervous silence."

"Well, don't forget, everybody. I'm taking private cases, as of now. If you ever need a nurse, just holler."

"If I ever have you for a nurse, I'll holler all right."

They were all ready now. Nothing left to do but go down and know finally and at last the airy touch of the organdy caps. In the auditorium, guests were moving down the aisles, turning their heads, this side, that side. On the stage, where many a doctor had stood to share his knowledge, flowers from the Sibert gardens were banked high and fragrant. A long table, piled whitely high with ribboned scrolls, stood back against the wall. Toward the front of the stage was a small table with pitcher and glass awaiting the speaker, and behind, to the sides, empty chairs destined for the Board.

The low voices murmured, greetings between people not lately met, bendings forward, around. Whispering.

Mrs. Joplin, privileged to be proud, smiled at Dr. Joplin, roundly happy beside her. Mrs. Bemis, placidly content, thought of tomorrow and home. Mrs. Gibson, with Archer at her side, thought how wise she'd been to have *this* hat made of roses—every eye was on her.

More and more heads turning around to the back of auditorium. When would they come? Were the seniors coming?

Nelle, Rosemary, and Gretchen met in the hall as they left their rooms. In the circling whiteness and forward surge, they stood a moment, linked, closer than they had ever been before, looking in each other's eyes.

"Well—I guess we're ready," someone said.

They moved apart.